girlfriend material

...

MELISSA KANTOR

DISNEP · HYPERION BOOKS
NEW YORK

First Edition
1 3 5 7 9 10 8 6 4 2

This book is set in 14-point Perpetua.
Designed by Elizabeth H. Clark
Printed in the United States of America

Library of Congress Cataloging-in-Publication Data on file.
ISBN 978-1-4231-0849-8

Visit www.hyperionteens.com

*To Julie L. Gantcher and
the memory of Neal I. Gantcher*

Chapter 1

I SWEAR MY MOTHER had been talking since Salt Lake City.

To appreciate how truly impressive a feat this is, you need to know that we were currently heading east on Route 6 toward Dryer's Cove, Massachusetts, almost three thousand miles from Utah, where our day had begun with a predawn drive to the airport. So officially my mother had been talking since *last night*. She'd talked in the car, she'd talked while we waited to clear security, and she'd talked during the flight attendant's demonstration of the plane's safety features, which means we could have been the first two people in history to survive a twenty-five-thousand-foot plunge into an open body of water only to die due to an inability to inflate our life preservers.

"Oh, Katie, this is just what I'd hoped it would be. We're *really* getting to know each other. Now, honey, smell the brine in the air? That's the ocean." Since my window was up, my mom took it upon herself to lower

1

it. My hair started flying madly around my face like it was attacking me. I took a rubber band off my wrist and gathered it into a ponytail.

"Mmm," I said. It was pretty much all I'd said since we'd left Mountain Time. My mother and I were engaged in a battle of wills in which she pretended (by throwing the occasional rhetorical question my way) not to notice I wasn't speaking to her, and I pretended (by occasionally humming a monosyllable in her direction) I wasn't not speaking to her. All of this because she'd yanked me out of my dream summer in Salt Lake City and dragged me across the country to be her companion in marital strife.

Every few months my parents' marriage starts to bear an uncanny resemblance to a *Desperate Housewives* episode. I come home to find my mom weeping into the phone, or I wake up on Saturday morning to the lyrical sound of my dad screaming, *What is it that you want from me, exactly?* Up until now I've just made it a policy to lie low (mostly by staying at my best friend, Laura's, house for days at a time) until the storm passes—an event that is usually marked by the appearance of several dozen red roses scattered in vases throughout the house, or the tinkling of a new bracelet on my mom's wrist.

This time around, things with my parents started heading south in early June, about two weeks ago, and as usual I fled to Laura's. Just to be clear, this doesn't exactly suck. Laura's house is practically a mansion, and she's got a pool and a hot tub, and except for the fact that her totally annoying brother, Tom, who's going to be a senior, and his totally annoying and *truly* idiotic friend Brad, enjoy spending their days blasting classic rock and arguing about football at the top of their lungs when Laura and I are hanging out in the pool, it's basically heaven at her house.

When I wasn't sitting poolside at Laura's, I was taking a summer fiction writing class for high school juniors at the U, and there was a lot of homework for that. Plus, Laura and I were playing tons of tennis at her tennis club because we both made varsity this year— only so did about ten other girls, which meant if we weren't kicking ass and taking names by September, we'd spend the season on the bench.

So aside from the fact that my home life resembled nothing so much as the beaches of Normandy on D-Day, I wasn't exactly having a bad summer, what with hanging out with Laura and getting in shape and writing stories and reading cool writers like Ernest Hemingway and F. Scott Fitzgerald. Plus, if past is prologue, I was pretty sure my parents would be all lovey-dovey by July 4th, and I'd be able to go home to do more than grab clean clothes.

Which is exactly what I was doing when I walked in the door two days ago and found my mother on the phone with her travel agent, talking about fares from Salt Lake City to Boston. I asked her what was going on, and she said, *I need to have some me time with Tina and her family on Cape Cod for the summer.* Tina was my mom's college roommate, and after college, Tina and my mom and Henry (Tina's husband) taught history in New York City together until my mom moved out West with my dad.

At first I thought she was just sharing information with me, like, *Honey, I want you to know you can reach me in Massachusetts until Labor Day.* You can see where I got this idea, right? What with the words "me time" featuring pretty heavily in her description of her plans.

My response was fairly mature, if I do say so myself. I didn't say, for example, *Well, Mom, maybe if you went back to teaching, since your kids are sixteen and twenty-one and therefore a* tad *old to need a stay-at-home mom, you'd be a little happier and less desperate for Dad's attention.* Instead I told her I was really sorry about things with her and my dad. I told her I totally understood her needing to get away.

I told her I'd miss her while she was gone.

But it turned out that by "*me* time," my mother meant "*we* time," and that it was not *one* ticket to Boston that she had purchased but *two.* That's when I completely lost it. I mean, my mom and I aren't even close. If she'd wanted my older sister, Meg, to go with her to the edge of the continental United States, that would have made total sense. Meg and my mom are peas in a pod where my dad is concerned. They love to sit around and talk about how insensitive he is and how he's so focused on his job he doesn't take time to appreciate Mom and how hard she works (?!?!). They especially love to say this while they're shopping online and charging it to his Visa.

When I suggested to my mom that maybe Meg could accompany her East, she said Meg was taking classes this summer (she's going into her senior year at NYU). *Oh, taking classes,* I said. *Who else do we know who's taking classes this summer?* My mom said it wasn't the same thing because I'm in high school and Meg's her favorite—oh, wait, no she didn't *actually* say that. She made up this whole thing about how the summer could be the perfect opportunity for us to "get to know each other better." Considering that my mom's idea of getting to know me involves asking if I'm really going to go out of the house in whatever it is I'm wearing, and telling me I have such pretty hair it's a shame I don't cut it more fashionably, this didn't exactly sound like a promise so much as a threat.

That's when I gave up on my mom and started begging my dad to let me spend the summer with him in Salt Lake. I reminded him that Laura and I had been playing tennis together every day so that we could be first singles this fall. I was sure that would convince him even if the whole writing class thing didn't. My dad's really into my being a great tennis player. He's the whole reason I started playing in the first place—when I was little, practically before I could walk, he had me out on the court hitting with him.

But it was too late: my father, like King Hamlet (which we read in English this year), had already had poison poured into his ear by my mother. He just said I shouldn't give my mom a hard time and there's plenty of tennis courts in Massachusetts and, *Sorry, honey, gotta go, I'm late for work.*

And there you have it, folks—writing class, gone. Kick-ass tennis game, gone. Summer with my BFF, gone. And why? So my mom could have some "alone time."

With me.

"I'm so excited for you to see Sarah again," said my mom. "Do you remember her at all from their visit?"

My mom was referring to this time around ten years ago that Tina and Henry and their daughter, Sarah, came to Utah on a ski vacation. I didn't really remember Tina or Henry, but I definitely remembered Sarah. She was awesome. She slept in my room and we spent the whole week playing really stupid tricks on our families. I remember once we hid about a million pieces of silverware in Meg's bed, and another time we put whole milk in the skim milk carton because both our moms were on this intense no-fat diet. But it's not what we *did* that's important, since most of it seems pretty stupid now. It's what it was like to be with Sarah. When I think back on that week, it seems as if we spent every second laughing our heads off. Sarah was hilarious. She was fun. She had these crazy frizzy curls that stuck out in every direction as if even her hair was having a good time.

She was like a party in a person.

Even though I would never in a million years have admitted it to my mom (and not just because it would have involved speaking to her), I was totally looking forward to spending the summer with Sarah. I hadn't spoken to or seen her since that visit almost ten years ago, but I had a feeling that wasn't going to matter, given how much fun we'd had the last time we were together. Now that we were too old to find sabotaging our mothers' after-dinner beverage of choice a satisfying evening activity, I pictured us having more age-appropriate fun, like driving around in her car (which I was sure was a convertible), going to parties with her cool New York private school friends, trading clothes, and talking about our futures together.

One of the books my writing teacher, Ms. Baker, assigned to us this summer was Hemingway's *The Sun Also Rises*. It's about this group of disillusioned and depressed twenty-somethings in Europe after World War I. All the main characters are men except for one— Lady Brett Ashley, who is without a doubt the coolest woman in the world. Basically, every man she meets falls madly in love with her because she is so beautiful and chic, but she doesn't care about any of them.

In Utah, I am exactly the opposite of Lady Brett Ashley. First of all, no guy has ever fallen madly in love with me. Second of all, unlike Her Ladyship, I do not have "curves like the hull of a racing yacht." I don't have a terrible body or anything, but I think my curves are probably more like those of a ferry or tugboat.

Third of all, I am not British aristocracy.

But ever since my mom had announced her determination to make me the Sancho Panza to her Don Quixote this summer, I'd been kind of thinking that maybe crossing the Mississippi would . . . I don't know, transform me. I imagined that Sarah and her friends were a little like the characters in *The Sun Also Rises*. (Not the depressed and disillusioned by the war part, but the having fun and going everywhere together part.) And if *they* were like *them*, then maybe *I* could be like Lady Brett, and maybe instead of having a *good* summer of writing and playing tennis and hanging out with my best friend, I could have a *perfect* summer of being chic and irresistible with a group of really cool kids from New York City.

Which, while I hadn't chosen it, was a trade I didn't exactly mind making.

EVEN THOUGH I HAVE my learner's permit, you have to be twenty-five to drive a rental car. When we'd left the rental agency, I'd been pretty bummed about the prospect of a summer with no driving, but now that I saw what driving ("driving") was like on Cape Cod, I didn't mind not sitting behind the wheel.

The road we'd turned onto when we left Route 6 wasn't really a road: it was more like a sandy driveway. Tacked up to trees alongside it were wooden signs with names on them. *Lipinsky. Charles. Boxer.* The signs pointed down roads that were, impossibly enough, even smaller and more overgrown than the one we were on.

My mom was driving at a snail's pace, and every hundred yards or so she'd suddenly jerk the car sharply one way or the other to avoid a hole or a tree root she hadn't seen until we were practically on top of it. I don't usually get carsick, but if we had much farther to go, I was definitely going to need to get out and walk the rest of the way.

9

Suddenly she let out a shriek. "I knew I'd recognize it!" she said, pointing at a fork in the road up ahead. A small official-looking sign on the left read, PRIVATE ROAD. NO BEACH ACCESS. Just above this, tacked to a tree branch, was an even smaller sign: COOPER-MELNICK.

As soon as I read the word *beach*, my mind was saturated with the image of me and Sarah driving home from the beach while our adorable boyfriends sat in the backseat, planning what to barbecue for dinner.

It was an image my mom's voice almost immediately dissolved. "I just hope you won't be intimidated by Sarah. I know she's a year older than you, and she's applying early to Harvard and all of that, but you bring *so* much to the table, honey. I'm sure she's really excited to have you as a buddy for the summer!"

Okay, *why* was my mother still talking? Because five seconds ago I'd been excited to see Sarah, and now she was making it sound as if Sarah was going to be *babysitting* me or something.

Suddenly my mouth felt dry.

My mom turned into the tracks and followed them for about a hundred yards. We crested a small rise, and then the house appeared almost out of nowhere. I'd been picturing, I don't know, a mansion or maybe some super-modern glass box, but this was an older, wooden building. Or I should say building*s*. We pulled up to what I guess was the main house, since it was much bigger than the other structure, which I realized from the shape was the garage. All the windows had window boxes that were practically bursting with brightly colored flowers. The whole setting was so beautiful and soothing that I was able to put my fears about Sarah out of my mind. It wasn't as if she'd never met me before. I mean, we were *already* friends.

And since when did my mom have her finger on the pulse of normal human relationships, anyway?

I heard a voice shout, "They're here!" as the front door shot open and a woman who had to be Tina came toward the car. A second later my mom had unbuckled her seat belt and then they were hugging. From the way the hug went on for longer than a hug hello normally does, and how Tina wasn't just hugging my mom but was patting her back and talking softly to her, I had the bad feeling my mom was crying. I took as long as I could getting out of the car, and by the time I was standing next to it, my mom and Tina had let go of each other. My mom's eyes were a little bloodshot, but if she'd been crying during the hug, she wasn't anymore.

"Katie!" said Tina.

"Hi," I said. I didn't know how to tell her that I haven't been called Katie by anyone but my family in about ten years.

"We're so glad you and your mom are here!" She said it nicely, like she really *was* glad my mom and I were invading their summer, then reached out and gave me a huge hug.

"Thanks for having us," I said.

It was funny to see my mom and Tina next to each other. My mom not only colors her hair blond, she wears it straight and kind of feathered back from her face, while Tina's curly hair has streaks of gray in it, and she didn't seem to have combed it that morning. Tina was wearing faded jeans with a hole in the knee and a tank top, while my mom had on a pair of crisp white pants and a pale pink sweater set. I could *not* imagine them as college roommates. Tina was so urbane, my mom so suburban. What could they ever have had to talk about?

The door opened and a man came out. Like Tina, he was in jeans and flip-flops. His hair had a little more gray than hers, and he wore hip, tortoiseshell glasses. Neither Tina nor Henry looked anything like any of *my* junior high history teachers.

"Hi," he called, walking toward us. "How was the trip?" A minute later he was hugging my mom, and I had the awful feeling that she was going to start crying again, but she didn't.

"We've met before, but it's been a long time. I'm Henry," he said, extending his hand to me. Like Tina, he seemed honestly glad to see us. "You must be starving."

"We stopped for lunch," said my mom. "But I

wouldn't say no to a snack. How about you, Kate?" Usually my mom calls me Katie. I figured maybe she was trying to send a message to Tina and Henry that they should call me Kate. It was nice of her to do that, since she knows I think Katie is a babyish nickname. Her trying to communicate that information to Tina and Henry without embarrassing me made me feel a tiny bit bad about how, basically, I hadn't spoken to her for the past seventy-two hours.

"Sure," I said, following the three of them into the house.

I didn't know what to expect from the interior of a house belonging to New Yorkers with "old family money" (which, according to my mom, was what Tina and Henry had). I wondered if it would be super chic with, like, only one piece of furniture in each room and enormous modern art everywhere; but it was nothing like that. We passed through a living room with big comfy-looking couches and pale wooden floors. There was a vase filled with fresh flowers on a grand piano, and a wooden rocking chair, but most of what you noticed were the books. One entire wall of the room was built-in bookcases, only even with all the shelves there wasn't enough room for the books. They were everywhere— the couches, the floor, even the bottom step of the staircase had a couple of ancient paperbacks stacked on it. I'm a total book junkie, so a house overflowing with books is basically my idea of heaven. I wanted to stop and see what the titles were, but Tina led us straight into the kitchen. It was sparkling clean and white, and it seemed to be all windows. There were enormous sliding-glass doors that led to a deck overlooking the water. Even on an overcast day like today, the room was dizzy with natural light.

As we sat on the deck eating brie-and-pesto sandwiches, I could tell that Sarah and her friends weren't going to be the only bright spot in my summer after all. Tina and Henry asked me tons of questions about myself, and when I mentioned that back in Salt Lake I'd been play-ing a lot of tennis because of wanting to be in good shape for the team in September, Tina said she was sure I wouldn't have a problem finding a regular game with someone. She said tennis is practically the official past-time of Dryer's Cove.

"And you had to give up your writing class," Tina said. "That was such a nice thing for you to do for your mom." She smiled at me and reached across the table for the hand that wasn't holding my sandwich. Then she gave it a little squeeze.

"Um . . ." I said. The combination of the beautiful house and view and Tina and Henry's enthusiasm for our visit and the delicious sandwiches was making me a little embarrassed about how ungracefully I'd behaved since my mom announced the change in my summer agenda. I wished Sarah would arrive so we could flee her parents and their guilt-inducing sympathy.

As if in answer to my silent plea, a car pulled into the driveway with a band I didn't recognize booming on the stereo.

Tina rolled her eyes, I guess at the volume. "That's Sarah," she said. "She worked a little later than usual today."

I was really surprised that a girl like Sarah, who went to a fancy Manhattan private school and had old-family money and a summer house, would have to have a summer job, but then Henry explained, "She's interning at the Dryer's Cove historical society. I'm sure she'll tell you all about it."

"Oh yes," said Tina, smiling at me. "She's *really* excited about your being here."

"Me too," I said, glad that Sarah felt the same way about seeing me as I felt about seeing her.

As soon as Sarah appeared in the doorway of the kitchen, I knew I'd been right about my chic summer with New Yorkers. She had on a pale green T-shirt dress that clung to her (perfect) curves. It was the kind of dress you'd see an A-list Hollywood starlet relaxing in while she takes the kids for a stroll on her private island off the coast of Tahiti.

For a second I was surprised by how different she

looked. She was a lot taller than I was, and her hair wasn't curly anymore; it fell in soft waves down to her shoulders.

"Hey," I said.

"Hey," she said, her back to me as she slid the door closed.

I don't know if it was her being so pretty or just the fact that I hadn't seen her in a decade, but I suddenly felt awkward. Was it okay to hug her hello?

My mom clearly wasn't having the inner dialogue I was. She pushed her chair away from the table and crossed the deck to where Sarah was standing. "Sarah, you've gotten so big," she said. "I can't believe how long it's been since I've seen you!"

"Hi, Jane," said Sarah. She didn't hug my mom back so much as she briefly draped her arms around her.

"Sweetheart," said my mom, turning around to face me, "don't you have that present for Sarah?"

For the first time since she'd arrived, Sarah actually made eye contact with me. I smiled at her, but she didn't smile back. It was hard to qualify the look she gave me, but something about it made me feel less like an old friend and more like a stain she'd discovered on an expensive item of clothing.

There was a beat of silence, and I realized everyone was looking at me. "Oh," I said. "Yeah, I do. But it's, um, packed."

Sarah, who hadn't seemed excited by the announcement that I had a gift for her, wasn't exactly devastated by the news that it was currently inaccessible.

"It's a shirt, just like Katie's," said my mom, forgetting, in her enthusiasm, not to use the nickname that made me sound like the six-year-old I'd been the last time Sarah and I shared a roof. "She thought you'd like something truly Utah!"

Now everyone was looking at my University of Utah shirt as if they expected it to do something emblematic of my home state (like maybe take a second wife or something).

Okay, for the record, when I'd bought Sarah a replica of the red T-shirt I was wearing, I hadn't gotten it for her because I thought it was *truly Utah*. I just figured, I don't know, it's a shirt I've had for a long time and it's faded in this fairly cool way, and I thought maybe Sarah might like to have a nice soft faded T-shirt, and *why was this suddenly such a BIG FRIGGIN' DEAL?!*

Incredibly enough, my mother was *still talking*. "Katie wears her shirt all the time. You'll be two peas in a pod, right?"

Sarah didn't say anything. Was it possible she just thought my mom's question was a rhetorical one?

"Honey, you're not working tomorrow, are you?" asked Tina quickly.

"Why?" asked Sarah. The way she glanced briefly at me before looking at Tina made me feel self-conscious   17 about my ponytail. Not that my hair exactly frames my face the way Sarah's blond tresses do, but at least when it's not up in a lumpy ponytail it doesn't make my head look like a mishapen bowling ball.

"I thought you could take Kate to the club, introduce her to everyone."

"It's supposed to rain," said Sarah. "Again."

"I heard it's supposed to clear," said Tina.

Okay, maybe I'd been misreading Sarah's behavior up until now, but I was most definitely *not* imagining how firmly Tina was talking to her daughter. If Sarah was, in fact, "so excited" to have me on Cape Cod, why was Tina talking to her as if money was going to be changing hands over me sometime before July Fourth. *Let's cut to the chase, Mom. What's my being nice to this girl with the tragic hair and total lack of fashion sense worth to you?*

"Well," said Tina, when Sarah didn't respond, "you two can go if it's nice out." It seemed to me I could actually see Tina clenching her jaw.

Sarah glanced up at the sky, where swirling clouds massed in the distance. A betting person might have been willing to play the odds that tomorrow would bring rain.

"Sure," said Sarah. "If it's nice out." She gave a little wave, like we were saying good-bye instead of hello. "It's good to see you again." Then she turned to go inside. "I've got to shower."

"If you're going to the movies with your friends," said her mom, "I'm sure Kate would love to join you."

Sarah pivoted in my direction slowly, not saying anything.

In the back of my mind I could still conjure up the picture of me and Sarah in her convertible, sun-kissed and tired from our day at the beach together. For a second it hung there, a perfect soap bubble suspended in thin air.

And then it popped.

It was kind of miraculous that I didn't start bawling right on the spot. Did she have to make it so humiliatingly obvious that not only did she have no interest in our being friends, she didn't even want to go to the movies with me? I mean, you don't have to talk to someone if you go to the movies together. You can just, like, sit there, staring at the screen and eating your popcorn. You don't even have to acknowledge the person.

Actually, Sarah was doing a pretty good job of not acknowledging my presence even as she was supposedly issuing me an invitation. She just stood there staring at a point slightly beyond my shoulder. For about half a second I thought I'd wait her out, force her to speak first, but never had it been clearer to me that I was outmatched. My words tumbled out almost faster than my tongue could form them..

"Actually, I want to unpack," I said. "But thanks for the offer."

19

"No problem," said Sarah. Nobody pointed out that there hadn't actually been an offer, and she walked back across the deck and slid open the glass door to the kitchen.

"Well," said Henry. He and Tina exchanged a quick look, and I saw him shake his head slightly. I hoped it was the kind of head shake a dad gives right before he grounds his daughter for the entire summer, not the kind he gives before resigning himself to some kind of *girls will be girls* philosophy.

"Well," Tina repeated, "why don't I show you the guesthouse?"

"That would be great!" said my mom, practically pirouetting with enthusiasm. "Last time I was here it was still the garage."

The garage? The *garage*?!

The path wound around the side of the house past a small fenced-in herb garden. The building Tina was leading us to was, in fact, the building I'd pegged as the garage—for good reason. It was roughly the width of two cars, and it had garage doors on it (though, now that I looked more closely, I realized they were made of frosted glass, not metal, as I'd originally thought). The flame of optimism that had been burning in me as I imagined my chic summer of love was officially snuffed out. It had been but a flicker of its former self after my meeting with Sarah. No way could it blaze bright in the face of the announcement that I'd be spending my summer sleeping in a garage.

But when Tina led us through a small side door, the garage we entered was nothing like our garage at home, with its outgrown bicycles and newspapers to be recycled.

The space inside was basically one big room with a couple of pale sofas and some comfortable-looking armchairs. There were bookshelves here too, though they seemed a little more organized than the others, like they were more for show than for use. The floor was blue tile, and there were large, brightly colored throw rugs everywhere. Just like at the main house, sliding-glass doors led to a deck overlooking the water.

Even though it was clearly a beautiful room, I couldn't help noticing that there were no beds in it.

"Both of these sofas open up," Tina said, as if she were reading my mind. "And there's a bathroom through that door right there." She pointed across the room. "I'm afraid there's not a lot of privacy, but you'll probably be in the main house most of the time anyway."

"Of course," said my mom. "It's beautiful." She looked at me, and I nodded. Now didn't seem like the right time to say I wouldn't have minded sleeping in an *actual* garage if it had meant I could have a door between me and my mother for the summer.

"I'm going to leave you to relax," said Tina, "and we'll

do a late barbecue so you can get some rest before dinner. Or we could go out if you prefer."

"Either sounds good," said my mom. I nodded again, too sad and tired to think of any other response, and Tina hugged us both before leaving.

This time *I* was the one who almost started sobbing on her shoulder.

"I'm so thrilled you're here," she said just before she shut the door.

"So are we," said my mom.

Sarah wasn't at dinner, so it was just me and the grown-ups. If I hadn't felt lame enough when Sarah dissed me earlier, I did now. My mood wasn't exactly lifted by the fact that after dinner, when my mom and I went back to the guesthouse, she couldn't stop going on and on about me and Sarah.

"You two were inseparable when they came to Utah. But *inseparable*. You followed her everywhere."

She was digging through her suitcase while I made up one of the sofa beds. How ironic that my mother, as it turned out, *had* had her finger on the pulse of my relationship with Sarah. I'd thought we'd been friends, but apparently I'd just spent that week following her around like the loser I apparently still was.

"I just know you're going to love being together again," she said. Her eyes were half closed, as if the idea of my friendship with Sarah put her into some kind of joyous trance.

"Sure," I said. "Whatever." For the millionth time I wished I was on Cape Cod with my dad and not my mom. My dad would never push me to be friends with someone who clearly despised me.

I left my mother to her reverie and headed outside, hitting Laura's number on speed dial even before my foot touched the wood of the deck. *Hey, it's Laura. You know what to do.* It was just a recording, but the sound of her voice made me feel like I wasn't completely alone in the universe.

"It's me," I said. "It's nine o'clock . . . No, wait it's . . ." Was it one hour or two hours earlier in Salt Lake City? "Well, it's nine o'clock here, and I think I'm spending the summer with the *hugest* bitch in the universe. Seriously, I might have to nominate her for *The Guinness Book of Records* or something. Call me."

Just a few hours ago, visions of best friends and beach barbecues and a summer romance had danced in my head.

Now I was living alone in a garage with my mother and her verbal diarrhea.

I hung up and plopped down into an Adirondack chair, still amazed by the speed at which my summer had gone from dream to nightmare.

Chapter 3

WHEN I WOKE UP at seven thirty the next morning, I knew it didn't matter if the Cape Cod–Salt Lake City time difference was one hour or two—no way was Laura awake at the crack of dawn on a Saturday. I rolled over and punched my pillows into a comfortable position. But even though I closed my eyes and tried counting backward from a hundred, when I got to one I was still wide awake. Not to mention starving. I looked over at the other sofa bed, where my mom was curled up on her side, fast asleep. I knew the second she woke up she'd start talking again, and I was so not up to hearing her continue to wax joyful at the prospect of Sarah and me becoming BFF by the Fourth of July. As stealthily as I could, I slipped into some clothes, grabbed my phone and a book off the shelf, and headed over to the main house.

It felt intrusive to slide open the door of a (relative) stranger's house and let myself in without announcing my arrival, but I didn't think Henry, Tina, or Sarah would appreciate my hollering *Hello!* at the top of my lungs when the silence that greeted me seemed like a pretty clear indication they were all still asleep. Even stranger was rooting around in their kitchen looking for breakfast stuff—I usually woke up before Laura, so I was always making myself breakfast at her house, but her kitchen and ours were the only ones I was used to rummaging through. It felt a little like snooping to be opening drawers and cabinets, even though Tina had kept telling me to make myself at home. I made a bagel with cream cheese and hustled out to the deck as quickly as if I'd been robbing the place.

Outside, I felt much more relaxed. It was really beautiful with the ocean so calm and the sun so bright but not hot at all. In Salt Lake in summer, you can definitely feel the heat by early morning.

I'd brought my cell phone out with me, and I called my dad. He's always up by, like, five a.m., even on the weekends, so I knew I wouldn't be waking him.

He picked up on the first ring. "Hey, kiddo, how's it going?"

"Okay," I said. Keeping my voice to a whisper, I told him how Sarah was about as psyched to see me as you'd be to see a staph infection.

He laughed. "I'm sure it's not as bad as all that."

"I don't know," I said, picking at the edge of my

thumbnail and peeling off a moon-shaped sliver. "Maybe you should just come and collect us now."

"Oh, honey," he said. "You should take advantage of this time. Relax. Enjoy!"

"I guess," I said, wondering what, exactly, I was supposed to be enjoying.

"Listen, baby, I gotta run. I've got a tennis game."

"Sure," I said, restraining myself from reminding my dad of all the tennis I wasn't playing due to my being exiled. "Have a good game."

"Thanks, sweetheart. Be good to your mom, okay?"

"Okay," I said, even though I was pretty sure we didn't see my mom the same way, what with his having chosen to marry her and all.

I hung up wondering how he expected me to act. Whenever Meg and my mom were together, my mom always seemed to have a nice time. It was like the two of them had this whole secret language or something. My mom and I, on the other hand, were clearly in need of one of those simultaneous translators the UN employs.

My dad telling me to enjoy myself reminded me of the last scene in *The Sun Also Rises*. Lady Brett and Jake, who's madly in love with her but who she's only kind of in love with, are in a taxi together in Madrid. Her latest love affair has just ended, and she says, *Oh, Jake, we could have had such a damn good time together*. And he says, *Isn't it pretty to think so?* I wished I'd just said that to my dad. *Oh, Kate, you should just relax and enjoy yourself!*

Isn't it pretty to think so, Dad?

I opened the book I'd taken from the guesthouse, an Agatha Christie mystery. It was so easy to slip into the world of village life in England that when the sliding door to the kitchen opened, I was a little surprised to raise my head and see I was actually on a deck overlooking a beach in America. I turned around, hoping to see Tina or Henry or even my mom. But of course it was Sarah.

"Hi," I said, folding the book over my index finger.

"Oh, hi," she said.

Sarah hesitated for a second, like she wasn't sure if she wanted to sit with me, then pulled out a chair two away from the one I was sitting in.

Neither of us said anything for a minute. When I couldn't stand the silence anymore, I said, "I can't believe how calm the ocean is."

Sarah glanced at where I was looking, then said, "It's the bay."

"What?" I asked, even though I: A) heard her, and B) know what a bay is.

"It's the bay," she repeated. "The ocean's on the other side of the Cape."

"Oh," I said. "Gotcha." *Gotcha.* I sounded like somebody's mom. Worse, I sounded like somebody's dad.

27

Okay, this had to stop. I might have lost our silent battle of wills over the movie yesterday, but I didn't have to yap away like some demented terrier. I opened my book again and sat staring at it, totally self-conscious, reading and rereading the same paragraph until the door slid open again and this time Tina came out. I turned to face her, dropping the Christie onto the table with relief.

"Good morning," Tina sang. She put her hands on Sarah's shoulders and kissed her on the top of the head.

"Hey," said Sarah.

Looking at them, I couldn't help sensing that despite their subtle bickering (clearly caused by the arrival of yours truly on their doorstep), they were a mother and daughter who liked spending time together, like they would have been totally cool with a cross-country trip that ended with their sharing a garage for the summer. I tried to imagine my mom standing with her hands on my shoulders. If she did, she'd probably only be doing it while she suggested I change something about myself, or tried to get me interested in some totally boring project of her own. *Since you're just sitting here, why don't we do something about what a mess your room is?* Or *I know it's July, but while we're both here with nothing to do, wouldn't now be a good time to talk about this year's Christmas photo?*

I mean, how are you supposed to get close to a person like that?

Tina reached over and gently ruffled my hair, then went back inside. A few minutes later I smelled coffee brewing, and I heard my mom's voice. She and Tina talked in the kitchen for a few minutes, but I couldn't hear what they were saying. Then the two of them emerged through the screen door, each holding a steaming mug of coffee.

"Good morning," my mom said to all of us. She pulled out the chair next to mine and squeezed my shoulder as she sat down. "Good morning, honey."

"Morning," I said.

"Just *look* at you girls," said my mom, taking in Sarah and me as if we were hanging on the wall in a museum.

"Can you believe we were ever that young?" Tina asked.

"You know," said my mom, looking at Tina, "I think I was exactly one year older than Katie is now when you and I met." Even though she hadn't yet said anything she shouldn't have, I couldn't help getting a bad feeling about where my mom's reminiscence was leading, which might have had something to do with how her voice was shaking slightly, like she was on the verge of tears.

I took a bite of my bagel, but fear of what my mother was about to say made it hard for me to swallow.

"And here we are"—she gestured at herself and at Tina—"and here *you* are"—she gestured from me to Sarah.

Now there was no way to hope that my mom was not headed over a cliff. But there was nothing I could do: one cannot prevent the inevitable.

A single tear slid slowly down my mom's cheek. "Here you are," she repeated. "The next generation of wonderful lifelong friends."

Tina put her hand on my mom's shoulder. "It's just crazy to think about," my mom concluded.

I could feel my cheeks blazing. I forced myself not to look at Sarah as I heard her chair scrape the deck.

"Isn't it crazy?" my mom asked of no one in particular.

"Crazy," echoed Sarah. But the way she said it implied the only thing that was even remotely crazy was my mother.

Was it any wonder I could not be close to this woman? When she wasn't forcing me to give up everything I valued and make my way across the country in some desperate attempt to get my father's attention, she was humiliating me in front of the only representative of my peer group for miles.

If my phone hadn't rung at that very second, I would have had no choice but to hurl myself off the deck and into the body of water I now knew was the bay. As it was, the buzz of the incoming call saw me leap out of my seat, mouth still full of bagel, shouting, "I've got to take this" even before I checked to see who it was.

I finally managed to swallow what was in my mouth. "Hello?" I said, heading off the deck and down the path to the guesthouse.

"You are not going to *believe* what I did last night," said Laura.

"Oh thank *God*," I said, looking over my shoulder to make sure I was out of earshot of the deck. "Thank God you called. I am in hell. I'm not kidding. I know traditionally they depict hell as this fiery underground cavern with little red men holding pitchforks, but it turns out hell is a woodsy summer community where——"

"I fooled around with Brad Lander last night!"

I always thought it was an exaggeration when characters in books describe their blood running cold, but now I actually felt it happen: my body temperature dropped several degrees. *"You what?!"* There was no planet on which I could imagine Laura fooling around with her brother's best friend, Brad. I'd only left Salt Lake City thirty hours ago. How had the universe as I knew it shifted so dramatically?

"Okay," she said, "I know you don't like him, but——"

"I don't *not* like him," I said quickly, thinking, I thought we *both* don't like him.

"He's really nice," said Laura. "He was telling me about how he misses his brother because they were on the football team together last year, and now that his brother graduated it just doesn't feel the same without him. And it was, like, sooo nice. He's really . . . I don't know . . ."

I forced myself not to supply the word *dumb*.

"He's just really . . . sweet," Laura finished. "I was hanging at home last night and totally missing you, of course. And he came upstairs because he thought Tom was supposed to be home, but naturally my stupid brother had screwed up and he was at the gym, so Brad and I just sat there talking for, like, an *hour*. And then he said he'd always kind of had a crush on me, only *he* thought *I* thought he was too much of a jock and everything, and then I said, 'I don't think that,' and then he said, 'Really?' and then he kissed me. And Kate, I'm not joking, he is *such* a good kisser. And we went outside and sat by the pool and he gave me his sweatshirt to wear because it was kind of cold, and he said he's totally going to explain everything to Tom and"—she screamed—"I just totally like him!"

"Wow," I said. "That is just so—" Brad and Tom had once held a contest to see who could hock a lugie farther across the pool.

Brad won.

"I know!" She screamed again.

How was this happening? How had my best friend gotten a boyfriend and I'd gotten . . . Sarah.

"So," I said, racking my brain for something to say

that wouldn't reveal how totally sorry for myself I was feeling, "are you—"

I had no idea how I was going to finish my sentence, so I didn't exactly mind when Laura interrupted. "The crazy thing is that he liked me this *whole time*," she said.

"That is crazy," I said, wincing as I remembered Sarah using the same word earlier.

Laura started listing all of the times Brad had noticed her without her *noticing* he was noticing her. There was the day she first wore her new black bikini. There was the time he'd watched me and Laura do handstands in her pool. There was the afternoon he and Tom had stolen an entire tray of chocolate-chip cookies Laura and I had baked and we'd called them both degenerate thieves.

The list, it seemed, was endless.

She continued narrating Brad's myriad but heretofore underappreciated good qualities, but I was too busy trying to figure out how to sound supportive to focus on the stories I was supposedly supporting. By the time I tuned back in, she was in the middle of explaining how Brad had managed to sneak into a second movie at Trolly Square after the one he'd paid to see had ended.

She's your best friend, I reminded myself. *She's your best friend, and if she's happy, you're happy.* "That's hilarious," I said. "Did he really do that?"

I heard my mom calling.

33

"Katie! Time to get ready to go to the club with Sarah and Tina."

Talk about being caught between a rock and a hard place.

"I'm really sorry, Laura, but I have to go. My mom's calling me."

"Nooo! Wait. Will you call me later? I have so much to tell you. And I want to hear about Cape Cod."

Well, my mom and I are roommates and she never stops talking, and the girl who I'm supposed to be best friends with has made it pretty clear she sees me as a pathetic leech who arrived to suck the fun out of her otherwise perfect summer.

"Sure," I said. "I'll tell you all about it."

I really wanted to be happy for Laura, and I wasn't exactly proud of myself for how I was feeling. But when you're embarking on what's clearly going to be the worst, loneliest time of your life, is it fair that your best friend in the world is setting sail for a summer of love?

Chapter 4

THERE WAS NOTHING SUBTLE about how my mom and Tina pushed me and Sarah to drive to the club together while the two of them drove in Tina's car; their whole *We have to run some errands on the way* was about as opaque as a plate-glass window. They hadn't thought of everything, though, and Sarah and I managed to go the entire drive without exchanging so much as two words due to her blasting the radio too loudly for even the briefest of chats. Attempt to prevent conversation, or preference about volume at which to appreciate Moby?

You be the judge.

I didn't really mind Sarah's not talking since I was so totally freaked out by the conversation I'd just had with Laura. I kept remembering this thing my dad had said to me back when I was in junior high and I complained to him about how stupid all the boys were and how none of them liked me or Laura. My dad was nice enough not to point out that these two things should have canceled each other out (i.e., if the boys were so stupid, why did

I care that they didn't like us?). He told me not to worry, that things would get better when we got to college, which is when guys get more interested in interesting women. I asked him if he thought maybe high school would be an improvement, but he said probably not.

Now, I have to tell you, when you're twelve, hearing that your life will improve when you're *eighteen* and that there's nothing but a romantic wasteland between here and "Pomp and Circumstance," is kind of depressing. But at least I'd thought Laura and I were in the same boat. I mean, she'd never had a boyfriend either.

Actually, for one brief second last fall it had looked like *I'd* be the one to prove my dad wrong. This senior had a big party, and Laura and I went with these other fresh-man girls, and I kind of hooked up with this guy Tim, who was in my year. I mean, we didn't, like *do* anything major, we just kissed. He was in my English class and I'd kind of thought he was cute when I met him—he went to a different junior high, so I'd only known him for a few weeks when we kissed at the party. And the thing was, and this is just so embarrassing I can't even believe I'm saying it, I kind of thought . . . I don't know, not that he was going to fall madly in love with me or anything, but that he'd want to . . . well, let's just say I didn't expect him to walk into English Monday morning and go *Hey*, and then completely ignore me for the rest of the year like he hadn't spent the better part of a Saturday night giving me a tonsillectomy with his tongue. A couple of weeks later he started going out with this other girl, and he and I basically never spoke again.

To cheer me up, Laura said we should make a list of all the things we *didn't* do that girls at our school who had boyfriends *did*. We didn't flip our hair around and giggle and squeal the second a guy came within a ten-foot radius of us. We didn't pretend we couldn't do our math homework without help from one of our male class-mates. We didn't spend every waking second wondering if what we were doing was attractive to the opposite sex.

Then we made a list of all the things we liked to do. We liked to read books and talk about them. We liked watching old movies. We liked being really, really good tennis players. We even liked when we could beat the guys on the tennis team. After we'd finished the list, we high-fived. No wonder the guys at our school didn't want to go out with us. Like my dad had said, we were waaay too cool for them.

But now it turned out that it wasn't that guys didn't want to go out with *us*.

It was that guys didn't want to go out with *me*.

I'd been expecting the Larkspur Golf and Country Club of Dryer's Cove, Massachusetts, to be really fancy, something like the Olympia Club in Salt Lake, which we don't belong to but Laura's family does. Olympia has valet parking and a brand-new clubhouse, inside of which pretty much everything is pink marble or brass. Larkspur, on the other hand, just had a dirt parking lot, and the clubhouse looked like an actual house, albeit a large Victorian one. There weren't too many of the Mercedes SUVs and BMWs and Hummers that you saw at Olympia, either. In fact, almost every car in the lot seemed to be a Subaru wagon. I had a minute to wonder how people ever found their cars when there were so many identical ones before I had to hustle to catch up with Sarah, who was headed down a pebbled path that had a hand-lettered sign saying "Pool" at the head of it.

As I followed Sarah, I felt not unlike a puppy struggling to keep up with a much larger dog. I swear, I wouldn't have been surprised if Sarah had said, *Hey, Kate, look over there* before dashing off in the opposite direction. As soon as we sat down, it was clear that despite our lounge chairs being next to each other, Sarah wasn't any more interested in talking to me poolside than she had been bayside.

I forced myself not to try and make conversation. If she didn't want to talk, that was fine with me. I opened the Agatha Christie again, trying to focus on the intricacies of a village murder and not the fact that my best friend had a boyfriend and the girl sitting next to me was probably hoping I'd drown in the pristine pool before lunch.

I'd barely made it through a sentence when I saw, out of the corner of my eye, Sarah shoot her hand up in the air and wave at someone. She was off her chair in a flash, though she did say something to me over her shoulder. It was either, *Excuse me a sec* or *Please be gone when I get back*. I kept my book up in front of my face as I watched her walk around the edge of the pool and embrace a shortish girl with a towel wrapped around her waist.

I was more relieved than I care to admit that Sarah didn't point over to my lounge chair and mime vomiting. This whole day was making me feel like I was going into junior high instead of junior year.

Okay, I had to stop. What did I care if stupid Sarah thought I was lame? I was only going to be here for at most two months, not the rest of my life. Starting tomorrow, I'd say I just wanted to hang out at the house. Was that such an awful way to spend the next eight weeks—sitting on Tina and Henry's beautiful deck and admiring the body of water I now knew was the bay? I could write. I could read. Let Sarah have her car and her club all to herself.

There was the squeak of flesh on rubber as a girl sat down on the lounge chair next to mine. I noticed Sarah hadn't left anything on the actual chair, just her bag at the foot of it. Should I say something about its being occupied? Clearly. But what was I supposed to say? *Excuse me, that's my friend's chair.* Hardly. *That chair belongs to a girl who hates me because I ruined her summer, which is*   39 *hilarious since I too am a victim of the world's vagaries rather than an agent in this affair.* Seemed a bit too much information to give to a complete stranger.

"Um, someone's sitting there," I said.

The girl was pretty, but not quite as pretty as Sarah; she looked more like the pretty girls at my school than a supermodel. Her hair was blond and straight and she had on a pair of jean shorts and a Princeton T-shirt. She was eating a peach, and some of the juice dribbled down her chin.

"Yeah," she said, swiping at the juice and wiping her hand on her shorts. "Sarah. I saw you guys come in. I'm Jenna."

"Kate," I said.

"I go to school with Sarah. You're the girl who's staying with her, right? You and your mom?"

What had Sarah told her friends about me? *You're not going to believe the loser my mom's saddled me with for the summer.* "Yeah," I said. "I'm the one."

"I've been to Salt Lake. My family goes skiing at Deer Valley sometimes," she said. Deer Valley is this really fancy ski resort that a lot of people from the East Coast and California ski at. When I ski with my friends, we usually go to Alta, which costs about half what Deer Valley costs. This may have something to do with the fact that at Alta they don't have tissues for you on the lift lines or heated seats on the chair lifts.

"So," she continued, "I'm sorry about your parents."

"My what?" I said, confused.

"Your parents? I'm sorry about their getting divorced," she explained.

"What?!" My screech could have cut glass. I cleared my throat and brought it down a notch. "Oh God, they're not getting divorced. They're just going through this *thing* they go through." What had Sarah said to Jenna to give her the idea that my parents were getting divorced? Could Tina have said something to Sarah? In which case, had my mom said something to Tina? My stomach started to wind itself in a tight knot as I imagined their conversation: *I don't want to say anything to Kate, but I'm going to ask Mark for a divorce.*

I forced myself to take a deep breath. This was insane. My parents were *not* getting divorced. No doubt Sarah and Jenna were just confused because they were used to New York women whose lives were just a little too busy for them to solve their marital crises by taking month-long cross-country vacations.

Jenna seemed to accept my response. "So," she said, "how do you like Cape Cod?" As she asked, she waved at someone. I assumed it was Sarah and the girl she was talking to.

You mean aside from your rumor-mongering friend? "It's nice," I said. "The air smells really clean." I took a deep breath, not sure why I'd chosen to utter this particular observation.

"Oh, I know," said Jenna. "I love how you can always

smell the ocean here. We've been coming up every summer practically since I was born."

We seemed to have exhausted our reservoir of small talk, so it was lucky that just then two guys emerged from the pool, dripping water, and stood at the foot of Jenna's lounge chair. They didn't spray us with water like the guys at my school would have, but I didn't know if that was because there was something intrinsically civilized about East Coast guys or if it was just that they didn't know who I was.

One of the guys was much hotter than the other. He looked as if maybe his great-great-great-grandparents had come over to this country on, like, the *Mayflower*, or as if he'd stepped out of a Ralph Lauren ad: chiseled jaw, blond hair that was long but not too long, piercing blue eyes. If you opened up a magazine and saw a picture of him playing polo, with the words "All-American" printed underneath, you'd definitely buy whatever he was selling.

The other guy was less obviously cute. He had dark hair and a slightly big nose, and while the first guy's body really did look like he played polo (in addition to working out ten times a week), the second guy's was what Laura and I call soccer-player cute—you know, like, *I'm in good shape, but my life's goals extend beyond the acquiring of six-pack abs.* Thinking about Laura reminded me of our phone call and that I was supposed to call her back, which, oddly enough, made me feel even lonelier than being surrounded by a group of total strangers

"Hey," said Jenna, looking up at the guys. "If you ˅ to play, we got an earlier court time."

"Oh, great," said the extremely cute guy. "Yeah, I definitely want to play."

"Me too," said the just-regular-cute guy. "But we need a fourth." The extremely cute guy gestured at Sarah's bag. "Where's Sarah?"

Jenna turned to me, which meant the guys turned to me too. It felt weird to have so many pairs of eyes on me. "She's over there." I pointed across the pool to where Sarah was still talking with the towel girl.

"Who's she talking to?" asked the extremely cute guy, squinting. "I don't have my contacts in."

"Victoria," said Jenna.

"Oh, great," said the extremely cute guy. "That's just what I need."

"Dude, you made your bed with that one," said the just-regular-cute guy, laughing.

"Dude, you *lay down* in that bed," said Jenna, also laughing.

The extremely cute guy shook his head and gave Jenna and the just-regular-cute guy the finger, but he was smiling a little too. "Screw all of you," he said.

"Actually," said Jenna, "we might be the only ones you *haven't* screwed," she said, and the three of them cracked up.

43

There's nothing like an inside joke to make you feel like a total outsider. I tried pretending that instead of being a loser with nothing better to do than watch three strangers talk to each other, I was eavesdropping in order to take notes for my next novel—the story of a group of deeply disturbed New York City private school kids who realize how empty and meaningless their lives are when they meet an honest, kind girl from one of the Rocky Mountain states.

I was deep in my *Oprah* interview when Jenna said, "Guys, this is Kate; she's staying with Sarah. Kate, this is Lawrence"—she pointed at the extremely cute guy—"and Adam." She pointed at the just-regular-cute guy. "And we are quite rudely washing Lawrence's *very* dirty linen in public."

"Hey, *my* linen's not what got dirty," said Lawrence, and they all laughed again.

Lawrence held out his hand to shake mine. "Nice to meet you, Kate," he said. I reached up and took his hand, trying to imagine a guy at my school shaking hands with anyone but a job interviewer. He had a good shake—firm but not like he was trying to show he was capable of breaking every bone in my body.

"Nice to meet you too," I said. He flashed me a super-model smile.

"Hey," said Adam. "Where are you from?"

"Utah," I said. Just naming my home state in front of

all of these New Yorkers made me feel like a hick. I should have lied. *Oh, I pretty much split my time between Rome and LA. You know how it is.*

"Cool, do you ski? My family rents a place out there every February."

"Deer Valley?" I asked. I wondered if he and Jenna were related or something.

Adam laughed. "No," he said. "Because, as you—a native—no doubt know, the skiing totally *sucks* at Deer Valley."

"Watch it, Carpenter," said Jenna, wagging her index finger at him.

"Sorry," he said, still laughing. "I meant to say that Deer Valley's *great*." As soon as Jenna looked away, he shook his head at me and made a face, scissoring his hands in front of his chest and mouthing *It sucks* to me. I started to laugh, which made Jenna look over at Adam, who quickly made his face neutral.

"Yeah," he continued as Jenna watched him. "I sure wish we skied Deer Valley. But we're an Alta family."

"You are?" I said, really surprised. "So are we. I mean, me and my friends. We ski Alta."

"So you never know," he said. "We might have skied together."

"We might have." I realized I was not only nodding my head but smiling at him. And was it my imagination, or had the day suddenly gotten a whole lot warmer?

"Well," said Adam, "it's nice to meet a fellow skiier." He extended his hand. "You know, a *real* skiier."

"I resent that," said Jenna. "If my boyfriend were here, he'd kick your ass."

I took Adam's hand. "Yeah," I said. As his fingers closed around mine, I felt a little pulse of something surge through my body. "It's nice to meet you."

I couldn't be sure, but it seemed to me that our eyes and our hands locked for a beat longer than necessary.

"So what's the deal?" asked Lawrence. "What time's the court?"

Jenna looked at her watch. "It's, like, now," she said. "Fifteen minutes. You guys should go change." She swung her legs over the side of the chair and stood up.

The three of them stood where they were for half a second or so, just long enough for me to imagine saying, *You know, guys, I play tennis!* They'd be amazed, then thrilled. I could see it now: I'd gather my stuff, and we'd all go off to the court. In my mind, the afternoon unfolded like a movie montage—Jenna and I having a friendly rally as the guys played a set or two. The four of us playing mixed doubles, Adam and I high-fiving as we beat Jenna and Lawrence. (Sarah arriving back to discover her abandoned bag on her abandoned lounge chair, then bursting into tears of loneliness and despair.)

Just as I'd gotten to the part of the evening where Adam asked me to go for a walk under the stars and confessed his undying love for me, Jenna said, "Well, it was great meeting you, Kate. I'm sure we'll see you soon."

"Yeah," said Lawrence. "Good to meet you."

"I'm going to go get Sarah," said Jenna.

"See you," said Adam.

It was nothing short of a miracle that I managed not to blurt out, *When?! When will I see you?!*

"Yeah," I said. "See you."

Once they'd left, I had nothing to do but go back to reading. I opened my mystery, but once again I found it hard to concentrate on Miss Marple's adventures. Only this time it wasn't because of Brad and Laura. Or Sarah. I put the Agatha Christie away and took out a pencil and my writer's notebook, which Ms. Baker had told us we should always carry. *You think you'll remember your ideas when you get home, but I guarantee that you won't.*

I flipped open the small pad and tapped my eraser against a blank page. The problem, I realized, was that I didn't have an idea for a story so much as I'd had an idea for my life. *All of Kate's dreams came true that summer when, shortly after she and Adam became a couple, Sarah had to return to New York for emergency surgery on the eardrums she had damaged by listening to excessively loud music as she drove.*

Did I really need to write that one down? Somehow I had the feeling I wouldn't forget it.

Chapter 5

SARAH CAME BY TO GRAB HER BAG, and that was the last I saw of her. I don't know why mobsters bother to off people when it's so easy to make someone *feel* like she doesn't exist. I ended up getting a ride home with my mom and Tina and spending the evening discovering, alone in my room, who done it.

Nothing like life in the fast lane that is modern teenage life.

Sunday morning, when I got up and headed over to the main house to get breakfast, my mom and Tina were sitting outside. I honestly didn't mean to eavesdrop, but before I could announce my presence on the bottom step leading up to the deck, I heard Tina say, "But is that any different from how it's always been?"

"He's just gotten so much worse," said my mom. "This is not what I signed on for when I got married."

The word *married* was hardly out of my mom's mouth when Tina saw me standing there.

"Morning, Kate," Tina said a little too brightly.

"Oh, good morning, honey," said my mom, turning around and smiling at me.

"Morning," I said. I noticed there was a box of tissues on the table between them, but it didn't look as if my mom had been crying. Maybe Tina just had hay fever or something.

Henry put his face up to the screen door but didn't open it. "I'm heading over to the club. Anyone want a ride?"

"No thanks," said Tina. "We're off to Provincetown."

"Kate?" asked Henry.

Another day being ignored by the Larkspur membership was a little more than I was prepared to handle. "Not just now," I said.

"If you want to go later, you can take one of the bikes in the shed," said Tina.

"Or you could come with us," said my mom.

"We're getting haircuts," added Tina.

"You could get one too," said my mom. "Maybe you want something a little more, you know, summer fun and flirty than what you have now?"

Because what I have now is so . . . what, winter despair and spinsterish? "Thanks, Mom, but I think I'll pass."

"Okay," she said. "Well, I'm going to go get dressed."

"Me too," said Tina, and she headed inside.

I wandered through the kitchen and into the living room in search of something to read. There must have 49 been two thousand books, almost all of which I'd never read, most of which I'd never even heard of. It was kind of intimidating. I took a book called *Lolita* off the shelf. It was by a guy named Vladimir Nabokov, and I'd at least heard of it, but I wasn't sure what it was about, just that it was supposed to be dirty or something. I opened it and read the first line. *Lolita. Light of my life, fire of my loins. My sin, my soul . . .*

"There's a great library in town."

I jumped about a mile, dropping the book in my surprise.

"Sorry," said Tina, coming into the living room. "I didn't mean to startle you."

"I was just . . . reading." I wondered if I should have asked before taking one of the books off the shelf, and I went to put it back.

"It's fine," she said. "Help yourself to whatever you'd like." She didn't check to see what I'd taken, which I thought was pretty cool. My mother definitely would have been all, *What are you looking at?* "But there's also a wonderful little library in town. If you're a book lover, you might like to browse there. It's very old school."

"I'd like that," I said.

Tina walked toward the kitchen, then stopped and turned around. "Hey," she said, "I meant to ask you this yesterday. I know it isn't exactly what we talked about when we discussed your wanting a regular tennis game, but would you be interested in giving tennis lessons?"

"I wouldn't be *not* interested," I said. "But I've never given a lesson before." I tried to picture myself telling some little girl to pull her racket back and keep her shoulder to the net like my dad used to tell me. It wasn't exactly brain surgery.

"Well, I'll give you the details, and you can decide. My friend's husband has been trying to give their daughter lessons, and it's been a little . . . tense. She was thinking maybe another teenager could reach Natasha better than her dad can."

"She's a teenager?" I'd been picturing someone about four feet tall who might mistake me for an actual grown-up.

"Well, just. She's thirteen. She's kind of a funny kid." Tina shook her head at something.

"Funny ha-ha or funny weird?"

"Ummm . . ." said Tina. Despite what she'd just said, I got the feeling she wasn't giving me *all* the details. "Let's just say that for what it's worth, I think she'd like you. She's really a nice girl who's going through a bit of a stage. We know the family from New York."

Tina crossed to a small table by the window and took a pad out of the top drawer. She wrote something on it, then held out a piece of paper. "Here's Carol's number," she said. "That's Natasha's mom. We didn't talk too much about money, but my guess is she'd pay you twenty dollars for an hour lesson."

Twenty dollars an hour?! I forced myself not to snatch the paper out of Tina's hand. "I'll call her," I said. "Thanks."

"No, thank *you*," said Tina. "Natasha's a really sweet girl. I think she could use a friend like you."

I decided to be flattered that Tina thought I could reach out to her friend's daughter, instead of insulted that she thought I could be friends with a thirteen-year-old.

When I turned on my phone, there was a new message on my voice mail. I hoped it was from Laura. *Oh my God, Kate, you're not going to believe this. Brad Lander gave me some kind of potion that made me think I liked him. Can you imagine?! Luckily I found the antidote, but I'm still pretty grossed out. Call me, okay?*

But it wasn't Laura, it was Meg. "Hey, little sister." Okay, I know I am, technically, Meg's little sister, but does she have to say it like she's forty years older than I am, rather than four? "I *hope* you're having a good *time*." Her voice had a singsong quality, as if she were speaking to someone who might still believe in the tooth fairy. "Mom said you're settling *in* and *adjusting* and every-thing, which is good because I *know* you were freaking out before you left." Read: *Because I know you're the most immature person in the universe.* "So *anyway*, I hope you're having fun in the sun and that we get to talk *soon*. Okay. Bye."

Ugh. I could *not* hit the delete key fast enough.

As I dialed the number Tina had given me, I was worried Natasha's mom would ask me all kinds of questions about my teaching experience, and I'd have to lie; but when I explained who I was, Carol just thanked me for taking on Natasha as a student (*a* student—like I had others!) and told me about ten thousand times that the biggest problem Natasha had was confidence.

"Sure," I said. "I know what you mean."

"Oh, you do?" said Carol.

Her asking made me wonder. Did I? I mean, I knew what confidence was, and I knew what it felt like not to have any. Maybe not on the tennis court, but definitely on the much bigger court we call life. Still, I wasn't sure Carol really wanted to hear that I believed I could help her daughter due to my having spent the past forty-eight hours as a social leper.

Luckily, the question had been rhetorical. "That's great," she said. "So would ten o'clock tomorrow work for you?"

"Yeah, sure," I said. *So would eleven or twelve or one or . . .*

"Wonderful. And is twenty dollars an hour all right?"

Considering that the most money I'd ever made in my life was nine dollars an hour to babysit these six-year-old twins from hell who live on our block, twenty dollars to hit a tennis ball back and forth (something I'd happily do for free) was way more than all right.

"Sure," I said. "That would be fine."

"Terrific," said Carol. "She'll meet you tomorrow at ten. I'll reserve a court."

The town of Dryer's Cove was so damn quaint, it was like a postcard come to life. There was a general store, a liquor store, an old-fashioned pharmacy, a bookstore, some antique and clothing shops, a penny candy store, half a dozen restaurants, and the library Tina had told me about. As I slid the bike into the bike rack in front of the library, I realized I'd forgotten to look for a lock in the garage; but then I noticed that none of the other bikes were locked up. Between the trust in their fellow citizens this indicated and the tiny, old-fashioned wooden building I was about to enter, I felt like I'd stepped back in time, to 1950 or something. The fact that I was wearing a vintage sundress I'd bought with Laura at this used-clothing shop we like only intensified the feeling that I'd been transported to another decade.

Even though I had only one hour of Monday scheduled, just having something to do the next day made me feel less lame for having nothing to do today. Wasn't that what Sundays were for: hanging around doing nothing?

I pushed open the door and found myself in a low-ceilinged, wood-paneled room. I took a deep breath, loving the familiar smell of books. There was a small annex off to the left with some large armchairs set up so their occupants could look out the window at the library's lawn with its charming gazebo atop a small hill. Straight ahead of me was a long table with newspapers and magazines spread out across it.

I'd expected the tiny library to just have mysteries and romance novels and other summer reading, and they did have that stuff, but they had a lot of classics, too. After wandering up and down a few of the fiction aisles, I found myself looking at *Lolita* again. Was it stupid to check out a book when there was a copy of it at Tina's house that she'd said I could borrow? Then again, it would be kind of nice to spend the afternoon sitting in that gazebo, reading and sipping an iced tea, and I didn't really feel like going all the way back to the house to get the book and coming all the way back to the library to read it.

The line to check out books was comprised entirely of the AARP set and me. When it was my turn to approach the desk, I tried exuding youthful enthusiasm for the tired-looking librarian.

"Do you have a library card?" she asked as I slid the book toward her.

I shook my head. "I just got here," I explained. "I

don't have anything." I gave her what I hoped was a charming smile.

She wasn't having any of it. "Do you have proof of residence?"

"Not exactly," I said. "I'm staying with my . . . with a family friend."

Her lips were tight. "Mmmhmm. Name?"

"Um . . ." Okay, how embarrassing was this? I couldn't remember if it was Tina Cooper or Tina Melnick. Or was it Tina Cooper-Melnick?

Someone had gotten in line behind me, and now he or she leaned forward slightly. I felt myself growing irritated with whatever senior citizen couldn't wait five seconds to check out the latest James Patterson novel. If I could just have had a minute, I might have managed to remember the name of my mom's oldest friend in the world, a woman who also happened to be my hostess.

Instead of backing up, the person behind me stepped even closer. "Don't believe a word she's saying, Barbara," he said. "This girl has book thief written all over her."

The voice was familiar. Very familiar. I turned to see the miracle worker who'd gotten the librarian to stop frowning.

"We have *got* to stop meeting like this." He was smiling like he was really glad to see me.

56   "Hey, Adam," I said, smiling back at him. He was

wearing a white Oxford and a pair of jeans, and he looked very definitely more than just-regular cute.

"So," he said, "trying to pull a fast one on the fine people of Dryer's Cove, are you?"

"I can't help her without any information, Adam," said the librarian.

As I was trying to imagine *any* of the guys at my high school being on a first-name basis with a librarian, Adam stroked his chin and looked me up and down. "She seems a reliable sort," he said. "I say, give her a card."

"It doesn't quite work like that," said the librarian. "The best I can do is let you check the book out for her."

"Hmmm," said Adam. "I guess I'd have to see what she's reading before agreeing to that." He reached over, took the book off the desk, and studied the cover. "*Lolita?!* I don't know. This is a pretty filthy book, young lady, banned in several of the more pious of these great United States."

I could feel my cheeks blazing. Why couldn't I have opted to check out *Little Women*? Now he'd think I was some kind of pervert.

Adam held the book up so the librarian could see it. "I have to admit, I'm shocked to see you, of all people, dealing in pornography, Barbara."

"Just give me the book, Adam," said Barbara, but she was smiling at him. Clearly I was not the only person in   57 the Dryer's Cover library who found Adam more than a little adorable.

"I'm just giving you a hard time," he said to me. "It's a great book. I read it last summer." He put a stack of what looked like comic books on the counter. "Can I give you these too?" he asked the librarian.

"Of course," she said.

"I wouldn't have pegged you for a comic book reader," I said. I was a little disappointed, actually. After he'd said that thing about reading *Lolita*, I'd assumed he was really into literature, but maybe he'd just had to read it for a class or something. Who knew what those New York private schools assigned for summer reading?

"Oh, these aren't for me," he said, shrugging in the direction of the books. "I'm doing an internship with low-income, at-risk kids at the community center. Today's Manga Sunday."

"Low income? There are low-income kids on Cape Cod?"

"Here you go, Adam," said the librarian.

"Thanks," he said, sweeping up the books under his arm. "Sure there are low-income kids on the Cape," he continued. "There's a year-round population here that's really struggling."

"And by struggling, you're not just saying they don't winter in Deer Valley," I said.

58   "Exactly," he said.

Without discussing it, we started walking toward the exit together. Adam held the door for me, then followed me onto the porch. We stood there for a minute.

I tried to think of something witty to say.

"Oh, here's your book," he said, handing me *Lolita*. "Sorry for giving you a hard time about it."

"That's okay," I said a little too quickly. "I mean, I didn't mind." Standing there on the porch of the library with our books and stilted conversation, it was like we really were something out of 1955. I smiled at the idea.

"What?" asked Adam, noticing my smile.

"This town's just so quaint," I explained. "I feel like one of us should say, 'Well golly, let's go get a pop!'"

Adam laughed and then, in a really enthusiastic voice, he said, "Golly, Kate, I'd love to get a pop with you. Would *you* like to get a pop with *me*?"

Okay, was he joking?

I didn't want to say yes if he was only joking. Then again, if I said yes and he *was* only joking, I could pretend *I'd* been joking too. But would it be obvious that I hadn't been? Maybe if I said yes with an accent. But I'm not really good at accents, and if he was serious, wouldn't it be kind of weird if I responded to a serious invitation by saying yes with some random accent?

It felt like about an hour passed with the two of us just standing there staring at each other, but maybe it was only a second or two before Adam added, "Unfortunately, I've got to get back to work."

"Oh, right," I said, surprised at how disappointed I was to hear him say that. "Of course."

"Take a rain check?"

"Definitely," I said. Was this a real rain check? Maybe it was a 1955 rain check.

The whole conversation was starting to give me a massive headache.

"Okay then," said Adam. "See you later."

"Later," I said. And as I watched him walk down the steps, I couldn't help hoping that "later" implied soon, and that the next time one of us suggested getting together, it would be clear that we were talking about doing it in the twenty-first century.

THE NEXT MORNING, as I was leaving the house for my lesson with Natasha, Henry warned me that you have to wear white on the Larkspur tennis courts. Luckily, I have a white tennis dress, so I put that on. As I got off my bike in the club's parking lot, I found myself looking around for Adam. But even though I'd come up with a bunch of (what I thought were) amusing one-liners for us to exchange, he was nowhere to be found.

Apparently he was too busy living his own life to be a character in the imaginary novel that was mine.

Larkspur's tennis courts were a thing of beauty. There were eight courts, all clay, and even though I thought making people wear white to play tennis was kind of a stupid rule, I had to admit it made you feel like everyone there was a serious player with a capital S. When I told the guy at the pro shop that a woman named Carol had booked a court for me and her daughter Natasha, he told me to go to court number three. Natasha's mom must have explained that I was giving Natasha a lesson, because he offered me one of the baskets of balls that real tennis pros always have.

Walking along the path that ran the length of the courts, all I heard was the steady *thwack!* of ball against strings. Normally that's one of my favorite sounds in the world, but today it made me a little nervous. Because I was teaching a teenager and not a kid, I felt like I couldn't just get away with doing the kinds of things my dad had done with me when I was first learning to play. I tried to remember my early tennis lessons, when I'd first started playing with someone other than my dad. I was pretty sure the instructors had us run back and forth across the court, doing something with our rackets, but I couldn't remember what it had been.

Now I was feeling something that definitely resembled panic. Natasha was going to show up, we'd say hello, then I'd . . . what, exactly? Even though she'd taught history and not tennis, I felt a sudden unprecedented respect for my mom. Had she been nervous, like I was, before her classes started? Or was it different if you had a lesson plan and stuff?

I took a deep breath and hitched my bag more firmly onto my shoulder. I was being crazy. I loved playing tennis. I was about to get *paid* for playing tennis. What could be bad? Natasha was going to be a great student. Maybe she'd recommend me to all of her friends. I could already see myself surrounded by an adoring crowd of my students, who would gather on the last day of the summer to present me with the #1 Tennis Coach mug they'd chipped in their allowance money to buy me.

When I got to court number three, I put my bag down by the bench outside the fence and walked the basket of balls onto the court. I felt a little stupid standing there not doing anything, but it seemed even stupider to start jogging in place as if I were about to play center court at Wimbeldon or something.

Luckily, before more than a minute or so had passed, a big beefy guy approached me.

"Are you Kate?" he asked. His face was red, and he had sweatbands on his forehead and wrists.

I nodded.

"Jim Davis," he said, extending his arm toward me. "Three-time club champion."

He said it like he was talking about the U.S. Open.

"Wow," I said as we shook hands. "Three times."

He was too proud of himself to detect the sarcasm in my words. "That's right," he said. He turned and looked over his shoulder. "And here's the next generation of Davis champions."

I looked where he was looking and almost dropped my racket.

First of all, the girl walking toward us was taller than I was. Significantly taller. This definitely put a crimp in

63

my plans to have her stare admiringly up at me as I dropped pearls of tennis wisdom into her eager young brain. Second, by the time she was within ten yards of me and her dad, I could see her scowling.

It was like even though we hadn't met, she already had a reason to be pissed off at me.

"Hi," I said, trying not to look as surprised by her appearance as I was. "I'm Kate."

"Hi," she said. She didn't smile, but she didn't need to for me to see that she had a mouthful of braces.

Mr. Davis put his hand on her shoulder. "This is Natasha," he said.

"Um, I think she knows that already," said Natasha.

"Now, Natasha," said her dad, "I want you to really show Katie here everything you've got, okay? I want you to just *dominate* this court."

Natasha rolled her eyes. I didn't exactly blame her; her dad already struck me as one of the more annoying samples of fatherhood I'd met in my life. Still, it wasn't my fault she had a lame dad. So why was she looking up (well, down) at me like her dad was only *one* of the annoying people she was being forced to deal with on this tennis court?

I made myself smile at her. "Let's get started," I said, though what I really wanted to say was, *Okay, first of all, nobody calls me Katie, Mr. Davis. Second of all, what's with the scowl, young giantess?*

I gestured for Natasha to go over to the opposite baseline from me, and then I went back to my side of the court. Right before I turned to face her, I was surprised to see that her dad had seated himself on the bench just outside the fence.

"Come on, honey," he shouted. "Let's see what you've got." He clapped his hands a few times.

I grabbed two balls from the basket and hit one lightly to her.

The ball landed almost directly midcourt before gently rising up just in front of Natasha. She bent her arm back at the elbow and wrist before swatting ineffectually at the ball, like it was an annoying or dangerous insect she needed to repel.

I was about to remind her to keep her elbow straight when a voice came from over my shoulder. "Honey, what are you doing? Is that how I taught you to hit the ball? You've got to be aggressive. You've got to *want* it."

"Gee thanks, Dad," she said sarcastically.

I wasn't sure how to interject my whole "pull your racket back" routine into their bickering, so I just hit another ball over the net. She swatted at it again.

"Oh, Natasha, what are you doing?"

I didn't know what to say. I mean, was I supposed to join Mr. Davis's chorus of criticism?

"Hey, Natasha," I said. "Why don't we switch sides? I think the sun's in your eyes a little bit over there." It was true that the sun wasn't *not* in her eyes on the far side of the court, but it was also true that maybe having her dad behind her would let Natasha relax a little. Of course, I wasn't sure what having to look at Mr. Davis would do to *my* game, but at least I was getting paid.

Natasha nodded and started heading toward the net, eyes on the ground. She walked hunched over, like she wanted to be about a foot shorter than she actually was. I had the urge to tell her to stand up straight.

Unfortunately, though Natasha could no longer *see* her dad, she was even closer to him than she'd been. I hadn't realized how much louder his voice was on the other end of the court, but when he opened his mouth again, the booming I'd come to associate with his running commentary was dimmed somewhat for me.

"What's the matter, honey? Why did you change sides?"

She turned to answer him, but I couldn't hear her response. His, however, was crystal clear. "What? *What?* Sweetheart, you can't be afraid of a little sun. Sun's not going to hurt you." Again the inaudible reply, but this time he didn't say anything in response, and the conversation ended.

"Natasha," I said, "I'm going to hit the ball to you. This time, will you pull your racket straight back from your shoulder, not from your elbow?"

She shrugged. I decided to take that as a yes, and hit the ball toward her.

To my surprise, she actually did what I'd told her to. There was the thump of a ball hitting the sweet spot in the center of the racket, then it was over the net. I'd pulled my racket back to return it when—

"Now that's what I've been talking about," Mr. Davis shouted, clapping his hands for emphasis. "*That's* what I want to see more of."

I don't know if Natasha was distracted by her dad's comment, or if she'd decided to punish him for his enthusiasm, but as the ball headed back toward her, she pulled her racket back from the elbow, bent her wrist, and swatted at the ball, which hit the frame of her racket and flew up into the air before landing almost directly at her feet and bouncing slowly into the net.

Lather. Rinse. Repeat. Each time I gave Natasha a suggestion and she followed it, her dad yelled something that made her furious and/or distracted her enough to ensure that she didn't do it again.

It was like trying to teach tennis with a Greek chorus sitting in the bleachers.

When the big clock by the pro shop read eleven, my dress was plastered to my body, and even with my baseball hat on, I felt as if the sun was beating directly onto my brain. It seemed impossible that the lesson had only lasted an hour: surely we'd been on this court since the dawn of time.

"Well, I guess we should call it quits for today," I

said, panting not unlike an overheated dog as I crossed to where Natasha stood. I'd waited until 11:02 so it wouldn't be too obvious that I was desperate to get away from bitter Natasha and her crazy father.

"Yeah, sure," she said.

"It was really nice to meet you," I said.

"You too."

Were we both lying? I knew I hadn't done a very good job of teaching her, but I couldn't see where I'd gone wrong. As Natasha's dad headed over to us, I wondered what a lesson with just me and Natasha would have been like. Not that I was ever going to have the opportunity to find out—no way was any sane parent going to continue to pay someone who clearly had so little to offer his daughter by way of tennis instruction.

"Thanks a million, Katie," he said. Then he reached into his pocket, took out a tight wad of bills and peeled a crisp twenty off the top. Given how much I disliked him, I wished I had the nerve to spit out something really insulting like, *Sir, you can keep your money.* But I just took the bill and thanked him.

"So," he said to me, "when's a good time for the next lesson?"

Was he serious? Did this man just have, like, money to burn? Did he not realize that his daughter was about as interested in learning the game of tennis as I was in . . . I don't know, hunting?

"Well, I . . ."

"Let's see," he said. "Today's Monday. Tomorrow we've got that sailing thing. Wednesday's the Fourth, so that's out. What about Thursday at ten again? Natasha?"

She shrugged. I couldn't tell if she was scowling at the idea of another lesson with me or if the look on her face was just her baseline expression of distaste for life in general. "Whatever," she said.

"Great. Does that work for you, Katie?"

Who was I to turn down twenty dollars?

"Um, yeah," I said. "Sure."

We said good-bye, and the second they were out of earshot, I dialed my dad.

"You are not going to *believe* the girl I'm supposed to be teaching tennis to," I said. I told him about Natasha.

"Sounds like she has a real chip on her shoulder," he said when I'd finished.

"Tell me about it," I said. I was sitting on the bench, zipping and unzipping the cover for my tennis racket. I was glad my dad agreed with me about Natasha's being a pain. Still, I *had* agreed to try and teach her again. "I don't know what I'm supposed to do," I admitted.

"I'll tell you what you can't do," he said. "You can't take responsibility for other people's anger."

"What do you mean?" I asked.

"I mean—hang on a second, hon." I heard him saying something to someone else. He sounded irritated with the person. "You know what, Katie," he said, "I'm really sorry. I've got to go and deal with this, okay?"

"Yeah, sure," I said.

"Honey, I wish I could solve this one for you. But just remember: you're the best. Anyone who doesn't appreciate that is just nuts."

"Thanks, Daddy," I said.

"I love you, Katie," he said.

"I love you too," I said.

Hanging up, I couldn't help but wish that, in addition to loving me, my dad *could* solve all my problems. I wished he could solve all of his and my mom's problems too, since that, actually, would have gone a long way toward solving mine.

Chapter 7

WHEN MY MOM HAD SAID she was going to get her hair cut, I'd figured she was going to do just that—get her hair cut. I hadn't expected to find myself on the latest episode of *Extreme Makeover: Mom Edition*.

I'm not exaggerating if I say that at first glance I thought she was Tina. I went home, put the bike in the shed, walked into the kitchen, and saw a woman who looked like Tina sitting at the table with a cookbook in front of her. I was literally about to say, *Hey, Tina* when the woman looked up at me and it was *my mom*.

First of all, her hair was dyed brown. I'd never seen my mom with hair even remotely resembling its natural color except in pictures from college and the early, early years of her marriage, like the ones where she and my dad are holding Meg in the hospital. Second of all, she hadn't had the hairdresser blow it out, so it was curly. Curly, like Tina's.

She stood up as I came in and walked around the table. On her feet was a pair of flip-flops like Tina's, and she was grinning a huge grin at me.

"So, what do you think?"

"Wow," I said.

"I know!" she said. "Tina convinced me to do it. Is it awful?"

"No, Mom, it's . . . You look great. Really." This was so weird. Why was my mother so interested in looking like Tina all of a sudden?

I was insanely relieved when just then the real Tina walked into the kitchen holding a huge paper bag with ears of corn poking over the top. It was way easier to look at her than my mom. "Henry brought the corn." She put the bag down on the counter. "He's off to play golf, but he dropped it off. Hi, Kate. Want to shuck?"

"I've never shucked before," I said, giggling a little at how dirty it sounded. "What's involved?"

Giggling too, Tina put her hand on my shoulder. "You always remember your first shuck," she said. "Let's make it tonight."

Actually, shucking corn isn't so bad. You rip off the husk and then there are all of these soft, silky threads that you have to peel away, and once you do you're left with a pristine ear of corn. In a little while, the bag on the floor between my legs was overflowing with strands of corn silk and empty husks, and there was a pile of bald corn on a platter next to me. The whole experience was very satisfying.

"So," said Tina, "how'd it go with Natasha?" She had a glass of white wine on the counter in front of her, and she was chopping garlic while my mom read through a cookbook. Apparently tonight was just a dry run for the feast we'd be having tomorrow, when Tina's brother, Jamie, arrived for the long Fourth of July weekend.

"Oh, yeah," I said. "I've been meaning to ask you about that. She's kind of—"

"Pissed off?" Tina finished, stopping what she was doing to look in my direction.

"Exactly," I said. "Pissed off. At *me*!" I added. "I mean, okay, her dad is such a jerk. But what did I ever do to her?"

"What's this?" asked my mom, looking up from a page that had a line drawing of a fish in a pan.

Now that I'd had a chance to get a little used to my mom's haircut, I didn't mind it so much. I told her about Natasha.

"What grade did you say she was in? Eighth?" asked my mom.

"I don't know," I said, turning and looking to Tina's back for an answer.

"She must be going into ninth," said Tina after a second. "Because her mom said something about her being at the high school next year."

I couldn't believe a girl who was only two grades behind me in school was supposed to take me seriously as an instructor. Maybe she was just resentful that her dad had hired some kid to teach her.

My mom shook her head. "Yeah, that's a tough age," she said. "When I was teaching, I always struggled with the eighth graders. They're tricky."

"Well, Dad said I don't have to take responsibility for her anger," I said.

Was it my imagination, or did my mom and Tina exchange a look when I said that?

"That's true," said my mom, and I was relieved she didn't say something negative about being married to my dad, like she had earlier on the deck with Tina. "You know," she continued, "you could try talking to her about stuff other than tennis. I remember sometimes I'd have a kid who was bad in history or just resentful about school in general, but once in a while if I got him talking about something else, we could connect over that."

"You mean, like, ask her what it's like to have such a major-league jerk as a father?"

My mom and Tina both laughed. "Well, I was thinking more along the lines of asking her about something she might enjoy discussing with another teenager. Boys, maybe."

In my mind I saw Natasha's hulking stance, the braces. "I don't know, Mom," I said. "I don't get a sense that there are too many boys in the picture." Not to mention how little my vast experience with the opposite sex would enable me to contribute to such a conversation.

"Okay," said my mom. "So you could ask her about her friends or school or what she likes to do in her free time. Just so she feels she can talk to you. If you two can relate to each other, you can teach her anything."

"You think?" I wasn't exactly convinced.

"I do," said my mom. "Anyway, what do you have to lose?"

"Good point," I said.

After that, no one said anything for a while. It wasn't bad sitting there in the kitchen with my mom and Tina, shucking corn. There was some jazz playing quietly, and Tina had started to cook the garlic, so the room smelled delicious. Maybe my mom was right—maybe it was just a matter of winning Natasha's trust. Maybe I really could help her, not just with her tennis game but with her confidence in general. Maybe by August she'd be a whole new person, full of life, smiling, joking, standing up tall. I could see her standing midcourt as the judges of the Larkspur Tennis Club handed her a trophy the size of a golden retriever. *And the winner of this year's club championship is none other than . . . Natasha Davis!*

We'd be like Annie Sullivan and Helen Keller!

It was cool to have a goal for the summer. And who knew—my giving Natasha lessons could provide an opportunity for Jenna and Lawrence and Adam to find out I like playing tennis, which could be the first step in their asking me to play tennis with them. It might even be an excuse to talk to Adam about teaching. I mean, clearly Natasha was not "at risk," what with her dad having a big fat wad of cash in his pocket and her going to a snazzy New York City prep school, but did "at risk" have to have only one meaning? Wasn't Natasha at risk of living a lonely, angry life? Weren't rich girls people too?

The phone rang. "Katie, honey, could you grab that? I'm up to my elbows in snapper," said Tina.

"Sure," I said, peeling strands of corn silk off my hands and shirt and walking over to the phone.

"Hello?"

"Tina?"

"No, this is Kate."

"Oh hey, Kate, it's Jenna. We met at the pool."

"Right," I said. "Hey."

The excitement I'd been feeling as I thought about changing Natasha's life (and her changing mine) translated itself into excitement about Jenna's calling. Maybe she was calling for me. I mean, if she wanted to reach Sarah, wouldn't she have called Sarah on her cell? In fact, maybe Adam had told Jenna to call me. *Jenna, you have got to call Sarah's hot, hilarious, houseguest and invite her to join us tonight.* Maybe he'd said, *I think I might be in love with her.*

"Is Sarah there?" asked Jenna.

And maybe not.

"No," I said, hoping my voice didn't convey my disappointment that she wasn't calling for me—or the humiliating fact that I'd thought she was. "Sorry," I added.

"That's okay," said Jenna. "When she gets home, can you tell her I have her cell? She left it in my bag. Will you tell her I'll bring it to Lawrence's later?"

So everyone was going to Lawrence's later. Well, it was always nice to know exactly where the party that you weren't invited to was. "Sure," I said. "I'll tell her."

"Thanks. Maybe I'll see you soon at the club?"

My disloyal heart swelled a little at the friendliness in her voice.

Traitor.

"Maybe," I said. I remembered how nice Jenna had been when she'd first sat down, like she was actually glad to meet me. Couldn't she beg me not to miss a day of sun and fun at the Larkspur country club? *Don't say maybe, Kate! You should* totally *hang with us tomorrow.*

"Okay," she said. "Well, thanks for telling Sarah about her phone."

"Sure," I said. "No problem."

I gave Tina the message and fled to the guesthouse.

Maybe Laura had been different the last time we'd talked, but she *was* my best friend. I hit her number on speed dial.

She picked up on the first ring. "Hey!"

"Can I just tell you how much my life sucks?"

"Oh my God, Katie, what happened?"

I launched right into the whole Sarah story. Laura's a 77

really good listener. She just said, *Oh, wow* and *Oh, no* a few times, but she didn't interrupt me. I was halfway through the scene at the pool when Laura said something I couldn't quite hear.

"What?" I said.

"Nothing," she said. "I was just talking to Brad."

"You were talking to Brad? Brad's there?" I suddenly felt really self-conscious about how long I'd been complaining.

"We're going to a movie in a minute," she said. "But finish your story."

"Um, okay," I said. But it felt weird to talk to her knowing she was sitting with Brad. Right when I finished, she said something else that I couldn't hear. "What?" I said again.

"I said, 'Stop it,'" she said, louder this time. Then she giggled.

"Maybe . . . maybe this isn't such a good time for us to talk," I said.

"No, no," she said. "It's a fine time. They sound like a bunch of spoiled brats."

That made me feel a little better. I liked the idea of Jenna, Lawrence, and Sarah sounding bratty. But what about Adam? I hadn't even told Laura about Adam.

"What?" said Laura.

"I didn't say anything," I said.

"No, Brad did," she said. I heard her muffled *What did*

you say? And Brad's even more muffled response. "Brad says you should tell them to go to hell and come back to Salt Lake City, where people don't suck."

Wow, Brad, that's such helpful advice. And I think you should let me have a five-second conversation with my best friend without offering up your pithy yet useless solution to my problems.

"Um, thanks," I said. "Tell him I'll keep that in mind."

"Seriously, Kate, you should just forget about those losers. Summer will be over before you know it. Don't make a sad face!" she added.

I was about to tell her that: A) I wasn't making a sad face, and B) even if I were, she wouldn't have been able to see it, when I realized she hadn't been talking to me.

The sound of a kiss confirmed my theory that it was Brad, not me, who was distressed at the thought that summer's halcyon days might swiftly come to an end.

"You know, I should go," I said.

"No, don't go," she said. "I want to hear more about what's going on with you. We haven't talked in days."

Even if Laura meant what she said, there was no way I could continue this three-way conversation. "I'll call you soon," I said. "I promise."

"I miss you," she said.

"Miss you too," I said. But as I hung up the phone, I had the feeling that even if I were in Salt Lake with her, I'd still be missing my best friend.

Chapter 8

WHEN I WOKE UP the next morning, my mom was already up and gone. I forced myself to sit on the deck and write. Ms. Baker had said that real writers write every day, and I hadn't written in almost a week. I kept thinking about Natasha and how angry she was, but I didn't want to write a story about an angry teenage girl. I could just see Ms. Baker or someone reading it and assuming I was writing about myself. I decided to write a story about a teenage *boy* who had some of Natasha's qualities, only the boy version of them. He'd be really short and skinny. He'd be scared of everything. I decided his family was going on a camping trip and he was supposed to have his own tent, only he was scared to sleep by himself. He thinks he's going to be eaten by a bear, but the dad just says, *There aren't any bears where we're going.* Maybe at the end the boy *would* get eaten by a bear. That seemed too obvious, though. Maybe he'd just see a bear and know his dad had been wrong?

When I finished the first scene, I thought it wasn't

too bad. I wished I had someone to show it to. When I'd told Ms. Baker that I wasn't going to be in the class anymore, she'd suggested that I find a group of other writers to work with for the rest of the summer. But what was I going to do, ask Sarah if she wanted to critique my prose? I could hear her now. *Actually, honey, I'd start with your wardrobe.*

I stretched my arms over my head; my back was really sore from sitting for so long. Plus, I was starving. I wondered what time it was. I decided I'd written enough for one day and headed toward the main house.

Henry was pulling some tough-looking weeds growing next to the steps. "Morning," he said, yanking on a huge stalk.

"Morning," I said.

"There's coffee," he said.

"Thanks," I said. I actually don't drink coffee, but I wondered if I should start. In *The Sun Also Rises*, Jake is always meeting someone for coffee before he goes to write up a story for the newspaper he works for. Then again, he often met them for several bottles of wine too.

Maybe it was a slippery slope.

"Sarah left for work already," he said.

"Oh," I said. Were our parents never going to realize that Sarah and I were just not going to be friends? "Okay."

"And I think your mom and Tina are in Orleans 81

getting supplies for the big dinner tonight." He mimed a drumroll. . . . "Uncle Jamie! But I can give you a ride to the club if you'd like."

"Thanks," I said. "I can just bike, though."

"Either way," he said.

Going to Larkspur didn't sound like such a bad idea. I could swim some laps or work out if there was a weight room. For a second I worried about running into Jenna or Lawrence and its being weird, but probably if that happened they'd just say hello and then ditch me. I made myself not think about running into Adam. He'd probably be at work anyway. I grabbed a swig of OJ and a bagel and headed out the door.

There was a bulletin board on the wall of the Larkspur clubhouse, and tacked to it was an enormous Xerox that read, "Stopping Lyme Disease Starts with You!" A huge drawing of a truly disgusting, engorged tick took up most of the paper, and around it were all of these warnings about not walking in the tall grass that bordered established paths and checking yourself and your pets on a daily basis. I couldn't believe people chose to vacation in a spot where every time you went for a stroll you were taking your life in your hands.

Not only was I never going to step off an established path, I didn't even want to step off the clubhouse *porch*.

I shivered and clutched my bag close to me like there

was a blade of grass nearby that it might brush up against and catch a tick from. Crossing the lawn to get to the pool suddenly felt a million times less appealing than it had a minute ago. I looked around at the overstuffed armchairs scattered around the wide porch and decided I'd just sit and read for a while.

I walked the length of the house, passing at least half a dozen adults reading copies of *The New York Times* and *The Wall Street Journal*. I had my eye on a sunny patch of porch at the other end of the building, and I'd almost reached it when a voice said my name.

I looked toward the railing, and there were Adam and Lawrence sitting on two of the overstuffed armchairs. Adam was looking up at me, and I felt my breath catch a little. I hadn't realized how much I'd been hoping to see him again.

"Hey," I said, glad my voice sounded normal even though my heart was beating really fast.

"Hey," he said. He pointed at Lawrence. "You remember Lawrence, right?"

Just how many people did Adam think I'd been introduced to since my arrival? "Right," I said.

"Hey," said Lawrence.

Then nobody said anything for a minute.

In *The Sun Also Rises*, Lady Brett is always running into guys she doesn't know all that well. When she sees them, she says, *Hello, chaps!* and they all go off to drink a Pernod together. But since I'm not exactly British, I couldn't really see myself addressing Lawrence and Adam as "chaps."

Plus, I don't even know what Pernod is.

"So how come we haven't seen you around?" asked Lawrence. He sounded genuinely bewildered, like he'd extended numerous invitations only to have me repeatedly RSVP *no*.

"Oh, I . . ." *Well, maybe if you or your friend Sarah ever told me I was welcome, I might have shown up more.*

I was still trying to figure out what to say when a voice behind me said, "Don't start in on me."

I turned around and saw Jenna coming up the stairs.

"You're late," said Adam.

"I'm ten minutes late," said Jenna. "Chill." She had pulled her blond hair back into a high ponytail, and was wearing a white tank top and a short blue skirt. "Hey," she said, seeing me. "Long time no see."

Once again I was at a loss for a truthful but decorous response. I just shrugged and smiled, as if I too was sorry I hadn't joined them more often but circumstances beyond my control had prevented it. Which, when you thought about it, was kind of true.

"So, are you guys ready?" asked Jenna.

"We've been ready for—" Lawrence started, but Jenna interrupted him.

84   "Dude, relax. It's not like you have a job or anything.

Adam and I are the ones deserving of some R and R."

I felt really weird just standing there. "Well, I should probably go," I said. "Nice seeing you all again."

"Do you feel like playing?" asked Jenna.

Even though she was looking directly at me, I couldn't believe this was an actual invitation. "Me?" I asked.

Jenna laughed. "Yes, you," she said.

"I think what Jenna means"—Adam leaned forward and looked me up and down in an exaggeratedly lascivious way—"is, would you be interested in a foursome?"

Because the last time the three of them had discussed a foursome in my presence, their conversation had included the words *court* and *time*, despite Jenna's wearing a blue (not white) skirt, I'd just assumed they were playing tennis again. What I hadn't realized, what hadn't even occurred to me, was that today they weren't talking about tennis.

They were talking about golf.

If you've never held a golf club in your life, you should know that the experience is totally counterintuitive. Holding a tennis racket feels like shaking hands: you wrap your fingers around the racket, and if it feels comfortable, you're probably doing it right.

Holding a golf club is exactly the opposite: you hunch over and grab the club with both hands wrapped around it in opposite directions. If it feels comfortable, you're definitely doing it wrong.

"That's great," said Jenna, observing my stance.

Adam looked over at us. "Wait," he said. Then he came over to me. "Hold your right hand a little lower." He reached down and moved my fingers around, and I could feel myself blushing beet red. "Now, pull the club back and swing all the way through, over the horizon."

"Okay," I said, even though I'd been too distracted by his touching me to listen to what he was saying. I lifted the club and felt a weird tension in my lower back, like I was moving a muscle in a way it was never meant to move. Then I looked up at the horizon and swung with all my might.

"That was good, that was good," said Jenna enthusiastically.

I looked around to see how far I'd hit the ball. It was nowhere in sight. I felt a surge of warmth and excitement. Maybe I was some kind of golf natural—could I have gotten a hole in one on my first try?

Lawrence nodded his approval. "Good swing," he said. "Good form." I got the sense he took the game of golf pretty seriously; when Jenna had suggested that I try one of his clubs since they were the lightest set, he responded as if she'd offered me a pair of his underwear—more specifically the pair he was currently wearing.

Adam knelt down and picked my ball up from the tee it had never left. "Practice makes perfect," he said, handing it to me.

I looked at him, truly amazed. "You mean I didn't even hit it? All that and I didn't even hit the ball?!"

"It's a really hard game," said Jenna. "I've been playing for years and I'm always making lame shots."

"That's true," said Adam.

"You have no idea," said Lawrence.

"It's practically taking your life in your hands to play with Jenna," said Adam.

"Sometimes they actually clear the course when she's coming through."

"Hey," said Jenna, "I believe the point has been made."

Lawrence bent down and put his ball on the tee, then chose a club from his bag and got ready to make his shot. I looked down at the ball in my hand.

"I didn't even hit the ball," I said.

Jenna put her hand on mine and squeezed it gently. "Don't overthink it," she said. "You'll just choke on the next hole."

"How many holes are there again?"

"Eighteen," said Jenna. When she saw the look on my face, she added, "But you'll be amazed at how fast it goes."

"So," I said, "how do you guys all know each other?" Jenna and I were looking for a ball I'd actually managed to hit, unfortunately in the exact opposite direction of where it was supposed to go. As we searched for it in the high grass that edged the green near the fifth hole, I silenced my fear of Lyme disease by focusing on the brilliant opening for a romantic interlude the universe had had the good grace to offer me. *Hey, Adam, when the game's over, would you mind if I asked you to check my body for ticks?*

"You mean besides all of us being in school together?" Jenna surveyed the grass around her as I did the same. "Well, Sarah and I have been friends for like, ever, so that's how I know her. And my boyfriend and Adam are really good friends, so I guess I started hanging out with Adam when I started going out with Biff."

Biff? She knew an actual person with the name Biff? I managed to hide my laugh with a cough.

"And we started hanging out with Lawrence last summer when he and Sarah were going out."

"Sarah and Lawrence went out?" Now I really *was* choking. Though, was it so surprising that the most gorgeous guy I'd ever seen outside of a magazine would have gone out with Sarah?

I just hoped his dumping of her had been brutal.

"Yeah," said Jenna, shaking her head (whether at what she was thinking or the ball she was [not] finding, I didn't know). "He was really psyched when they got together. But she just wasn't into it. They still fool around sometimes, but I don't think she'll ever be his girlfriend again."

"But I thought . . ." I stopped.

"What?" Jenna looked at me.

Was it weird that I'd been listening to their conversation that first day? I mean, they *had* been talking right in front of me. "I thought Lawrence got with a lot of girls. He seemed like—"

"A slut?" offered Jenna.

Slut is a word I always associate with girls. "Can a guy be a slut?" I asked.

"They can, and Lawrence is," said Jenna, and we both laughed. "But it's kind of tragic. I think he's still into Sarah." Suddenly she let out a scream of triumph. "Found it!"

"Oh, you totally rock!" I said. As we high-fived, I felt psyched about way more than the ball we'd just found. She'd told me about her, Sarah's, and Lawrence's love lives.

But she hadn't said a word about Adam's.

Later, as the four of us were sitting by the pool drinking lemonade, I started to get a little nervous about Sarah. I had no idea what time she had to work until. What if she stopped by for a late-afternoon swim and found me hanging out with her friends? It wasn't like I thought she'd stand there, hands on her hips, going, *Okay guys, it's*

Kate or me. Choose. Still, wouldn't her arrival make things a little . . . chilly for me?

Nobody had said anything for a few minutes when Lawrence asked, "So what's the plan?"

"I'm thinking your house, I'm thinking movie, I'm thinking clam strips, and I'm thinking seven thirty," said Adam.

"Done, done, done, and done," said Lawrence. "But we pick the movie. I'm not watching another crap chick flick."

"Oh, please," said Jenna. "You'll watch one and you'll like it."

"Adam, I need you to back me up on this."

"You're man enough to handle a chick flick," said Adam, his eyes closed against the afternoon sun. I didn't want to be caught looking at him if he opened his eyes, so I forced myself to refill my lemonade from the pitcher.

"I want to watch an old movie," said Jenna. "Hitchcock or something."

"Oh, you should rent *Notorious*," I said. It was practically the first sentence I'd uttered all day that I hadn't played over in my head first. Talking without planning felt surprisingly good.

"Excellent call," said Adam. "We're watching that."

Right at that second I remembered the list Laura and I had come up with—things we liked that girls who had boyfriends didn't. *Playing tennis. Reading and talking about books.Watching old movies.*

I couldn't help noticing how many of those things Adam and I had in common.

"It's almost five," said Lawrence to Adam. "We've got that court." He stood up, and so did Adam.

"I should get going too," said Jenna, checking the time on her cell phone. "The tide is high." She sang a few bars of the Blondie song, which was apparently meant as an explanation of her destination; but what exactly the song was supposed to explain remained opaque to me.

"What happens when the tide is high?" I asked.

"Oh, I'm doing this internship at the Audubon center," said Jenna. "We're charting the salinity of tide pools."

"I can never understand how you're so interested in something that doesn't involve people," said Adam.

Even though I thought it was cool that Jenna had such an unusual-sounding internship, I had to agree with Adam. If I had a summer job studying something, I'd want it to be people.

"I'm interested in people too," said Jenna. "For example, I'm going to call Biff before I go."

"Aah," said Lawrence, "monogamy. It's so beautiful." His tone indicated he found it anything but, and I wondered if Jenna was wrong about his having a thing for Sarah.

Jenna reached over and hit him on the side of the head. "Don't knock it till you've tried it." She looked around to make sure she hadn't forgotten anything, then took a step away from the table.

"So we'll see you guys around seven thirty?" she said.

For the second time that day it took me a minute to realize she was talking to me.

"Ah, yeah," I said. "I'll, um, tell Sarah."

Now *there* was a conversation I was looking forward to. *Hey, Sarah, Jenna said we're supposed to be at Lawrence's at seven thirty. And by "we're," I mean you and me, honey.*

"Great."

"See you tonight," said Lawrence. He put down his drink and stood up.

"See you tonight," said Adam, grabbing the lemon wedge from his glass and standing up too.

"Yeah," I said. "See you tonight."

"I look forward to it," said Adam.

It wasn't a full-body tick check, but it was a start.

Chapter 9

MAYBE MY DAD HAD BEEN WRONG about my having to wait for college to have a guy like me. Maybe there *were* guys who I could be into and who could be into me, only they all lived in a different zip code. It was kind of an exciting prospect, and the whole time I was riding my (well, Tina's) bike home from Larkspur, I kept thinking about seeing Adam at Lawrence's house later.

As I stepped into the cool of the shadowy living room, I saw Sarah lying on the sofa reading *The New Yorker*.

She looked up as the screen door slammed shut. "Hey," she said, lazily turning the page.

"Hey," I said. I'd already decided to make my announcement quickly—just rip off that Band-Aid. "Um, I ran into Jenna and those guys today," I said, hoping my rabid joy in their company didn't show.

"Yeah, Jenna told me," she said, not looking up from her magazine. "I just talked to her. She said you played golf with them."

"I did," I said. I almost added *It was fun*, but a second

before I did, I wisely reminded myself that Sarah was not my parent. "They, ah, said . . ." I couldn't bring myself to utter the word *we,* as in, *we are invited*, in case Sarah looked me straight in the face and said, *Who's "we," exactly?* so I just finished, " . . . they're meeting tonight at Lawrence's at seven thirty."

"Yeah, she told me," said Sarah.

Was I going to have to ask her permission to go? Was I going to have to ask her for a ride? Was I going to have to get a ride from someone else? It occurred to me that I not only didn't know where Lawrence lived, I didn't have any of their phone numbers, so it wasn't like I could call and ask.

Why was Sarah making this so difficult? "So I . . ." I wanted to scream. I wanted to yank her perfect blond hair out of her head by the roots. I wanted to grab the magazine from her hands and force her to eat it, column by column.

Finally Sarah looked up at me. "My uncle's coming up from New York, so my parents are cooking this big dinner. I already told them about it."

Of course. Uncle Jamie! How could I have forgotten about Uncle Jamie?

Whom I suddenly wanted to murder.

For a split second I had the crazy idea that I'd go to Lawrence's house anyway. After all, *my* uncle wasn't coming up from New York. But just as I was imagining showing up at Lawrence's (wherever that was) solo, having biked over, Tina came out of the kitchen.

"Hey, Katie, did you have a good day?" she asked. She was holding her hands in front of her at an odd angle, but before I could ask why or answer her question, she said, "I'm dripping scallop. Are you two ladies ready to lend your youthful energies to this fabulous family feast?"

Sarah groaned, and in the midst of my despair, I actually felt a tiny sliver of solidarity with her in her irritation.

"Sure, Mom," she said. "We're ready."

I was halfway to the kitchen when I realized that, ironically, Sarah had just used a word I'd been unable to utter only a few minutes earlier.

We.

Maybe it was because Sarah kept referring to him as Uncle Jamie, but I'd gotten some idea that Jamie was Tina's older brother and that he was actually elderly or at least oldish. When the car pulled into the driveway, I expected Henry to walk in the door with a gray-haired man in a suit.

But Jamie turned out to be Tina's younger brother, and he was wearing a pair of ripped, faded jeans, a T-shirt, and a pair of hip-looking sneakers. I'm not into older guys, but if I were, I would definitely have thought Jamie, with his shoulder-length brown hair and light blue eyes, was cute. He came and gave everyone, me included, a huge hug, and when he got to my mom, he made a big deal out of lifting her slightly off her feet and swinging her around.

"I can't believe you're here," he said. "It's so great to see you again." He was still hugging her, which bugged me. I mean, the woman *did* have a husband who just happened to be my father.

"You too, Jamie," said my mom, and I was glad she extricated herself from his hug as she said it. "It's just great seeing you."

Tina hadn't been exaggerating—dinner really was a feast. In addition to ceviche, Henry and Tina had prepared salad and grilled vegetables and cooked up a ginormous pot of linguine with clam sauce. They'd even made their own bread. I was so stuffed by the time Tina put a second serving of pasta on my plate, I felt like the tick from the poster.

I'd anticipated spending the entire night being pissed about not getting to hang out with Adam, but for a while it was actually fun being with Sarah's family. It was even okay being with Sarah. Maybe it was because we were the only people under thirty sitting at the table, but at one point when her mom referred to "rap music," Sarah said, "Mom, it's *rap*, not rap *music*. You're, like, the poster child for lame." She rolled her eyes and made a face in my direction that indicated I'd understand what she meant, and we both laughed.

By the time Henry uncorked a third bottle of wine, I couldn't help noticing that my mom and Jamie seemed happy to see each other. Really happy. My mom kept calling Jamie "Coop," which apparently had been his nickname in high school, which is where he was when she had first gone home with Tina for a vacation and met him.

"I had such a crush on you," said Jamie, and it took me a minute to realize he was talking about my mother. "You walked in the door with that green suitcase—"

"Oh God," she said, "I'd completely forgotten about that suitcase."

Jamie reached across the table and poured her some more wine. We were sitting out on the deck, and Tina had put several candles in glass holders on the table. I wished the setting didn't feel quite so . . . romantic. "Okay," said Jamie, "how much does it prove my eternal devotion that I remember the suitcase?"

"Utterly," said my mom, laughing. "Utterly."

"And then you ran off to Utah. To *Utah*, for Christ's sake." He shook his head as if it was beyond his ability to fathom the absurdity of my home state.

My mom's cheeks were flushed. She doesn't normally drink very much, but she took a sip of the new glass Jamie had poured her. "I never stopped missing the East Coast," she said. She looked out over the water. "My God, how did I end up there? I'm a New Yorker."

97

This was news to me. In all of my sixteen years of life, my mom had never so much as once uttered a word to indicate she felt at home anywhere but where she lived: i.e., Utah.

"Do you ever think about coming back East?" asked Jamie.

Suddenly there was something truly insidious about this conversation. I mean, who was Jamie to ask my mom if she thought about moving East? How about asking her if she and *her husband* ever thought about moving East?

I waited for Tina or Henry to say something to him. Maybe, *Okay, Jamie, that's enough. I think you've had a little too much to drink, and it's fueling a trip down memory lane that nobody but you wants to take.*

But neither of them said anything. They were just watching my mom and Jamie smile at each other as if they didn't know my mother was a happily married woman.

"I'm stuffed," I said abruptly.

You would have thought the sound of her daughter's voice might have made my mom a little embarrassed to be flirting like a teenager, but she didn't even look my way.

"I think I'll turn in, actually," I said a bit more loudly than I'd announced the state of my stomach.

"Sure, honey," said my mom, finally looking at me. I
tried to make my eyes say, *You're freaking me out,* but my

mom was apparently unable to read eye-speak.

"Good night, sweetheart," said my mom.

"Good night," said everyone else.

The last thing I wanted to do was leave my mom alone (i.e., unsupervised by me) with Jamie, but now that I'd announced to the table my intention of going to bed, it would have seemed a little weird to suddenly go, *Actually, I'm staying right here.* The real problem was that what I wanted was not to go to bed myself but for my mother to go to bed.

Alone.

Since I wasn't in the least bit tired, I walked away from Tina and Henry's and just sat in the dark on the deck of the guesthouse. Then I called my dad.

"Hello?" he said. I could hear people talking in the background; it sounded like he might be at a party or a restaurant.

I cut right to the chase. "Dad, you have to make up with Mom. She's, like, flirting with Tina's brother."

I hardly expected my dad to hang up immediately in his mad dash to get to the airport, but I definitely didn't expect him to just laugh and go, "Oh, Katie," like I was eight and had just told him I wanted a pony for my birthday.

"Don't 'Oh, Katie' me," I said. "Did you hear me? She's flirting. With another man."

"Well, a little attention from the opposite sex never killed anyone," said my dad. Then he said, "So, how're the lessons going? That girl's father still a problem?"

It wasn't that I wanted to be my parents' marriage counselor or anything, but did my dad really not care at all that his wife was almost three thousand miles away from him, listening to some guy recite an ode to her college suitcase?

"Dad, I hate to sound like a broken record, but Mom's—"

"Honey, I told you to drop it, and I was serious, okay?" His voice was sharp.

"Sorry," I said. I thought he'd say he was sorry too, but he didn't. Then he asked me how everything was going, and I just said, "Okay." I really didn't feel like talking to him anymore, so I told him I had to go, and we said good-bye.

I felt awful when I hung up the phone. My dad had just basically told me to shut up. My mom was flirting with another man.

Just a month ago I'd actually thought we were a reasonably happy family.

I didn't want to be alone with my thoughts, but I didn't want to call Laura either. Here's who I didn't feel like having advise me on my family situation: Brad.

Practically before I could think about it, I found myself dialing Meg's number. I got her voice mail. *This is Margaret Draper. I'm sorry I can't take your call right now. Please leave a detailed message after the beep, and I'll get back to you as soon as I can.* Was my sister the only college junior whose outgoing message made her sound middle-aged?

"Hey, it's me," I said. "Um, Mom's being really weird. She, like, got her hair cut, and she's totally flirting with Tina's brother. I don't know. Will you please call me?"

As soon as I hung up I was sorry I'd called. I could already imagine how Meg would condescend to me when she called back. *Kate, you just don't understand Mom very well. I'm sure she wasn't flirting. Why don't you focus on your life and let Mom worry about hers.*

As I sat semi-stewing on the deck in the dark, I heard the side door of the main house open and shut. A minute later Henry said, "It's great to have Jamie here, isn't it?"

"I guess," said Sarah. "Not like he's talking to any of us."

Henry laughed. "He does only have eyes for Jane, doesn't he? Well, it's nice for her. She's had kind of a rough time of it."

"I guess," said Sarah again.

I heard a noise I couldn't identify and then the sound of bottles rattling together. I realized they must have been putting the garbage into the bins.

"Kate seems like a nice girl."

Clearly they thought I was asleep. Either that or they

didn't realize how far their voices carried in the still night. My heart started pounding, and I tried to make myself as small as possible in my chair.

I could practically hear Sarah's shrug.

"Have you invited her to the Fourth of July bonfire at the club yet?" asked Henry.

"I'm sure she won't want to go," said Sarah. "She doesn't know anyone."

Henry's voice had just the slightest edge to it as he said, "That's why you'll introduce her to people."

There was a pause and then Sarah said simply, "Fine."

Henry said something else, but I couldn't hear it, and then the door swung open. "Dessert, guys," called Tina.

"Coming," said Henry, and I heard them walking across the gravel. A second later the door slammed shut.

I knew Henry meant to do me a favor. I knew he was a nice guy who wanted me to have the chance to party with my peers as we rang in another bright year of our fair republic.

There was only one problem with his strategy: now that I knew Sarah had been forced against her will to invite me, there was only one thing I could say to her invitation:

No.

Chapter 10

MY MOM CAME IN at one in the morning. I'd finally fallen asleep only to be woken up by her and Jamie giggling at the door. If you haven't been awakened in the middle of the night by the sound of your tipsy mom giggling her head off with some guy who's crushed out on her, all I can say is you'd better hope you never are. For a minute I had the horrible thought that she was going to invite him in, and I was torn between: A) flipping on a light to remind her that, *Hello! Maybe instead of acting like a teenager, you should remember that you* have *one,* and B) feigning REM sleep so I wouldn't have to interact with my mom and her . . . whatever, when I heard her say, "Good night, Jamie," in this way that made me think maybe he'd wanted their evening to continue. She shut the door, and I heard her humming quietly as she headed to the bathroom.

When I woke up at seven, I couldn't stand the idea of trying to be quiet while my mom slept off her wine, but the thought of going over to the main house and possibly having to talk with Jamie was even worse.

Since I didn't want to deal with anyone, I decided to go for a run. I got dressed, grabbed my iPod, and headed out the door and down the narrow sandy path through the grass that led to the beach. The mist and the dark clouds actually made me smile.

Have fun at your barbecue, Sarah . . . in the rain!

Even though I knew (thanks to Sarah) that I was looking out at the bay and not the ocean, I understood how I'd been confused. Maybe on a clear day you could see that this body of water didn't stretch all the way to Europe, but with the clouds and fog, the feeling that there was no land as far as the eye could see was impossible to shake. I set off, trying to stay close to the water's edge, where the sand was tightly packed and easier to run on.

Salt Lake City is surrounded by mountains, the Wasatch to the east and the Oquirrhs to the west, so I'm used to looking up and seeing them whenever I run. During tennis season, when I run with the team, it's daytime, and they're shadowy and green with the afternoon sun, but in the summer, when I run alone, usually as the sun's going down and as it's getting cooler, they're lit up bright pink against the dark blue of the evening sky. I guess being surrounded on all sides by mountains could make a person claustrophobic, but it always made me feel safe.

The water was having the exact opposite effect on me. Every time I looked over and saw its flat, gray surface, I felt sad. Maybe it was because of the mood I was already in, but something about the vast expanse of water seemed so . . . lonely. Technically there were probably fishermen and scuba divers out there, just like in Salt Lake there were skiers or hikers up in the mountains, but instead of making me feel less isolated, like in Utah, the thought of all of those faceless people going about their (aquatic) business just made me feel more alone. I ran for half an hour and then turned around and ran back.

Halfway through the return trip I passed an elderly couple. They were studying a stick or a feather that the woman was holding, but at the sound of my footsteps on the sand, they looked up and waved.

Through the music playing on my headphones, I heard the man say, "Morning," and the woman said, "Good morning." They smiled at me.

"Good morning," I said, and then they both waved, and I waved back.

I guess it was objectively a meaningless exchange, but something about how friendly they'd been to a total stranger made me feel less alone. As I trekked through the fine dry sand of the dunes toward the house, I looked around and saw the crisp green sea grass waving in the wind against the slate gray of the sky, and it all struck me as a little more beautiful than it had just an hour before. I breathed in deeply, feeling the briny air sink into my lungs. My legs were tired, and it had been long enough since my last run that they were starting to ache from the strain, but it was a good ache.

My sense of contentment would, no doubt, have faded eventually, but seeing Sarah headed down to the beach along the same path I was headed up made it disappear faster than a bug scuttling out of the way of an approaching shoe. I could have stepped to the side to avoid her, but the path was about six inches wide, and tall beach grass grew up along either side of it.

I wasn't about to get Lyme disease just so Sarah could get to the beach faster.

"Hi," she said, clearly surprised to see me.

"Hi," I said. I was glad I'd caught my breath down on the beach and wasn't still panting from my run. My voice was cool, collected.

Sarah was wearing a pair of running shorts and a jog bra, and her hair was up in a high ponytail. "Did you just go for a run?" she asked.

Considering I was wearing sweat pants and running shoes and that my face was, I knew, bright red and drenched in sweat, I didn't see what else she thought I would have been doing. *No, Sarah, I'm just back from enjoying a leisurely cup of coffee.* Yesterday I might have felt obligated to say something about how I liked running on the beach or how long it had been since I'd worked out, but remembering Sarah's irritated "Fine" from last night, I wasn't in the mood to make small talk.

"Yeah," I said.

"I'm going for one now," she said. "I'm supposed to be training for field hockey, but I've been kind of lazy about it."

"Oh," I said.

My terse response seemed to unsettle her. "So, I was going to invite you to the Fourth of July barbecue at the club tonight," she said.

Oh, I bet you were, I thought. But I didn't say anything.

Now my silence was definitely making her nervous. She ran one hand up and down her thigh a couple of times and bit her lower lip. "But it looks like it's going to rain."

I looked up at the sky. In fact, the gray looked a little lighter than it had an hour ago, as if the sun might actually break through after all, but I didn't say that. In fact, I didn't say anything.

"So I don't think they'll have it. If it rains, I mean."

"Probably not," I said. I liked the effect my failing to utter more than two consecutive words was having on her.

"Um, are you like, pissed at me or something?" she asked. For the first time since she'd seen me coming up the path toward her, Sarah looked directly at me.

I always say no when people ask if I'm mad at them. If you say yes, then you have to say why you're mad, and that usually involves getting into something you'd rather not get into; whereas if you say no, the thing you're mad about usually passes without some big awkward confrontation. Plus I think people want you to say no when they ask if you're mad at them. I mean, if someone thinks you're mad at them, you probably are, and if you're mad at someone, they probably know why, and the only reason they're asking is because they feel guilty about whatever it is they did, and they're hoping you're not going to confront them. Once they've asked, they can feel all superior, like, *Well, I* asked *her if she was mad and she said no, so what was I* supposed *to do?*

Even though I knew what she was doing, I couldn't bring myself to tell her the truth. *Yes, Sarah, I* am *mad at you actually. And you know why? Because from the second I arrived in your time zone, you've made it crystal clear that I'm what stands between you and a good time.*

"No," I said, hating myself. "I'm not mad."

"Oh," said Sarah. "Good." She looked up at the sky. "Well, if it doesn't rain later, you should come to the barbecue."

This was my moment.

Like I'd ever accept *an invitation from you, Sarah.*

Like I even want *to come to your stupid party.*

And then I heard the following words come out of my mouth: "Great. Sure."

Sarah slipped her headphones into her ears, and we sidestepped around each other.

I like to think that if I had lived at a time when tremendous bravery was called for—in Nazi Germany, for example, or in the South before the Civil War—I would have been one of those people who risked her life in order to do the right thing. That I would have hidden Jews in my attic or helped slaves escape along the Underground Railroad.

I like to think that.

But I have the bad feeling it might not be true.

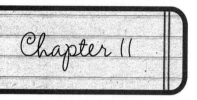

Chapter 11

AS IF IT WERE ON MY SIDE, the weather held for the rest of the day. It never completely cleared up, but by the time I headed over to the main house to go with Sarah to Larkspur, the sun was making a truly valiant effort to poke its way through the clouds, and not a drop of rain had fallen since morning.

I'd spent the day trying on and rejecting outfits. I kept telling myself, *You don't even know if Adam will be there. Maybe he's a vegetarian with a moral objection to barbecues. Maybe his parents make him stay home every Fourth of July and read the Constitution out loud to them.*

But no matter how many times I told myself not to get my hopes up about seeing Adam, I couldn't stop their hovering just above the stratosphere.

Even if I hadn't wanted to wear something that would make Adam notice me, I would have faced a major fashion dilemma. The problem was, I had no idea what to wear to a Fourth of July barbecue at a place like
110   Larkspur. If we had been going to the Olympia Club, it

would have been easy—even when people just go to play tennis or swim, they can barely lift their arms because of all the jewelry they're layered in, and when Laura had her sweet sixteen there, and the invitation said "festive casual," I bought a fancy new dress and so did my mom.

Maybe fancy was the way to go. Just because the Larkspur population wasn't particularly bejeweled didn't mean they weren't the type to get dolled up to celebrate our nation's birth.

I'd only brought one real dress with me, a strapless wild profusion of purple and red flowers with a stiff crinoline under it. For a minute I wondered if crinoline + sand = major catastrophe, but slipping the dress over my head and feeling its smooth, stiff bodice glide over my shoulders erased that fear. I spun around. The dress was sooo pretty. Adam just had to be there to see me in it.

Satisfied with my wardrobe choice, I took off the dress and went to shower, and when I got out, I saw that Meg had called me back; I'd completely forgotten about the message I'd left her. The message on my voice mail was typical Meg. She was *so sorry* she'd missed me, and she was *sure* I'd misunderstood Mom's behavior, and this was *such* a hard time for everyone, and blah blah blah blah.

I barely listened to the whole thing since I'd realized in the shower that I had a major shoe dilemma on my hands. The high-heeled red sandals I'd bought to go with the dress were going to be kind of hard to walk in on sand, even sand that had been packed hard by the morning rain. I put on the dress and slipped on the sandals. They were really high, and I felt unsteady just crossing the room. I took them off and put on my flip-flops—maybe together they'd look all elegant yet sportif! I went over to the mirror to check out the combination.

Disaster.

I took off the flip-flops and put the shoes back on. It wasn't like I was going to have to walk miles or anything. They probably had waiters and stuff to bring food to your table.

I checked myself out in the mirror. The dress was low-cut without being tacky, the three-quarter skirt coy yet sexy.

I looked like a total New York girl.

Or at least I thought I did.

Right up until I saw an actual New York girl.

When I walked into the living room, Tina and Henry were lying on the couch, each of them reading a section of *The New York Times*. I'd said hello to Jamie, who was puttering around in the kitchen, and I tried not to let the delicious smell of tomatoes and garlic emanating from whatever he was cooking make me nervous about his ability to get with my mom. Why did Jamie have to be cute, crushed out on her, *and* a good cook?

"Don't you look pretty," said Tina, looking up. Henry nodded his agreement.

"Thanks," I said, heading to the foyer to wait for Sarah.

And then she came downstairs, and I knew I'd made the fashion mistake of a lifetime.

Sarah was wearing jeans rolled up at the ankles and a tiny black T-shirt with cap sleeves. It looked as if she was going to one event and I was going to another.

"Um, hi," she said.

I could feel my face blazing.

"Hi," I said. No way was I staying in these clothes if everyone else at the barbecue was going to be dressed like Sarah. I waited for her to make a crack about what I was wearing, but she didn't say anything. Finally I couldn't take it anymore. "I guess . . . I thought I should get dressed up."

I could already hear her response, *Well, you thought wrong.*

There was a pause, then she said, "It's probably okay if you wear that." Surprisingly, she didn't say it in a snotty way, like, *It's* probably *okay if you wear that. I mean, if you want to win the club's annual biggest loser award.*

I thought about what she said. The key word seemed to be *probably.* "Do you think other people will be dressed like me or like you?" Oh God, could I trust her answer? 113

"Honestly?" she asked. She was looking me up and down, but her gaze was more measured than critical.

I nodded.

"I think it's a really pretty dress, but you'll probably be more dressed up than most people."

It wasn't until I'd exhaled that I realized I'd been holding my breath. "Would you mind waiting while I change?" I said.

"No problem," she said.

I'd unzipped the dress and tossed it to the floor even before reaching the bureau, where my favorite jeans were folded in the bottom drawer. They're ancient, ancient Levis, and I bought them at the same store where I got the sundress I'd worn to the library, so they had already been perfectly worn in the first time I put them on. I threw them on then snatched a pale green tank top out of the same drawer. It was a split-second decision, but I hoped it was a good one since I've always thought a tank top says, *Who knows, I might be sexy* but not in an obvious or slutty way. As I was racing out the door, I slipped on my flip-flops.

The whole time I was getting dressed I kept muttering *Thank you, thank you, thank you* under my breath, and I was halfway back to the main house when I realized the person I was thanking was Sarah.

114   She was sitting on the arm of the sofa when I entered

the living room, and she nodded at what I was wearing.

"Way better," she said.

The sprint to and from the guesthouse combined with the instantaneous costume change had left me a little breathless, but I managed to say, "Thanks." Then I smiled at her and she smiled back at me, and it felt almost as if we'd jumped back in time, crossing over all the exchanges we'd had this summer to arrive at the week we'd spent in Salt Lake being friends.

"You girls should probably bring something warm to put on," said Henry. "It's going to get cold later and it might rain."

"Talk about ruining a look, Dad," said Sarah.

"Suit yourself," said Henry. "Kate, I hope you're more practical than my daughter. There are plenty of sweaters in the closet. Or you can take a sweatshirt."

Jeans were one thing. Jeans and a sweatshirt were another. I shook my head and Henry shrugged.

"They can stand the cold," said Tina, not looking up from her paper. "They're young."

When the front door opened and my mom walked in carrying a cake box, I was relieved to see that she was wearing jeans and a sweatshirt. How intent could she be on seducing Jamie if she was wearing that?

"Have a great time," she said; and for the first time in the history of our relationship, she didn't make a comment about what I was wearing to a party.

"Thanks," I said. And even though I meant it only in the most limited way, I said, "You too."

I followed Sarah out to her car, wishing the last thing I heard as the screen door shut behind me hadn't been my mom saying, "Do I have time to change before dinner?"

All the other kids at Larkspur were dressed like Sarah and me, and the adults were dressed equally casually, in fleeces and other clothes you wouldn't have been surprised to see at a campsite or an Albertson's. A few of the men were wearing old-man slacks with actual animals on them—one gray-haired guy we passed had on blue pants with a turtle pattern. A couple of the women had on diamond engagement rings, but none were dripping jewels.

Just imagining having worn my dress and heels was enough to make me want to bend down and kiss the hem of Sarah's jeans in gratitude. I was so thankful to her I didn't even mind that my ears were still ringing from the volume at which she'd blasted Jonathan Richmond and the Modern Lovers on the way over.

There was a buffet table not far from where we entered the beach, and a bar was set up nearby. Most of the older people were standing in the vicinity of the bar, holding drinks and talking in groups of five or six. About a hundred yards away was a bonfire, and that's where

most of the little kids were—running around and

screaming for no real reason, the way kids do. I scanned the crowd for Natasha, not especially surprised when I didn't see her. She hardly struck me as a run-around-at-the-barbecue type.

Lawrence was standing, his back to the water, literally surrounded by girls. Jenna stood a few feet away from Lawrence and his harem. Adam was standing with her, and I felt a little tingle of something between happiness and relief wash over me at the sight of him.

"Hey," called Jenna when she saw us coming. Adam looked up too. He had on jeans and a gray long-sleeved T-shirt, and there was a sweater tied low on his hips. In my humble opinion, it was a very sexy look.

The word Hemingway sometimes uses to describe Lady Brett Ashley is "jaunty." Walking down to meet my friends (or people who weren't *not* my friends) and a guy who I had a crush on and who might possibly have a crush on me, I felt a bit jaunty myself.

As we approached them, Jenna said, "You're just in time for the Lawrence show." We all looked at Lawrence and the girls. I wondered if he really didn't notice that Sarah and I had arrived, or if he just wanted Sarah to see how many girls were into him. If the latter, I felt a little bad for him, because Sarah seemed not to care very much.

"I'm starving," she said. "Let's leave them to their fate and eat."

We left Lawrence talking to the girls and made our way over to the tables of food. I'd never seen a feast like this one—there were dozens of lobsters, hundreds of mussels, thousands of scallops. Huge bowls overflowed with fresh peeled shrimp next to which sat boats of cocktail sauce. At first I felt a little self-conscious about eating in front of Adam, but my first run in a week had left me starving. I was relieved to see Jenna and Sarah pile their plates full of food, and I filled mine too. Then the four of us found a spot in the sand a little away from the crowd, right at the base of the dunes. Despite the clouds swirling around, there was enough sun that the water was too dazzling to look at.

Sarah was the first of us to be done. She stood up and brushed the sand off her butt. "I want to go see who else is here," she said. "Anyone want to come?"

"Sure," said Jenna, standing too. "If we can get seconds on the way." She swallowed her last bite of shrimp. "You guys want to come?"

"I'm good," said Adam.

I really wanted to be alone with Adam, but if I stayed, would it be obvious that I wanted to be alone with Adam? Then again, was I really going to leave the guy I was crushed out on and go for a walk just to make it seem like I didn't have a crush on him?

"I'll hang out here for a little," I said.

"See you guys later," said Sarah, and she and Jenna

headed off in the general direction of the buffet table.

I looked out over the crowd, which had grown while we'd been sitting down. "I feel like I'm observing an unknown tribe," I said. "These people could not be less like the people I know if they tried."

Adam lay down and folded his arms under his head. "Think of them as the local aborigines."

"They might as well be," I said. "I've never seen anything like them before. They're so . . . understated." Lots of the women had actual gray hair, another thing you don't see much of where I come from.

"Is this your first time here?" asked Adam.

I wasn't sure if by "here," he meant the East Coast or Massachusetts or Larkspur. I decided to interpret it as Cape Cod. "Yeah, my first trip."

"Are you having fun so far?"

Laura and I once took this quiz in *Cosmogirl!* or girl.com or something. It was called "Are You a Good-Time Girl?" and was all about, like, are you willing to try new things and do you make guys feel happy to be with you because you're always in a good mood? I didn't exactly fail, but when I got my score, it advised, *Try to be more enthusiastic and to maintain a positive attitude—it's surprisingly attractive.*

"I *am* having fun," I said after what I hoped wasn't too long a pause. And it wasn't like I was lying. I mean, was

I having fun when I had dinner with a man who seemed determined to seduce my mother? No. Was I having fun when I tried (and failed) to improve the tennis game of the angriest girl in the world? Not so much.

Was I having fun now, sitting with Adam on a beach? *Ding, ding, ding, ding, ding.* Score.

"I'm getting to read a lot," I added.

"How are you liking *Lolita*?" he asked. He'd rolled over onto his side and was squinting in the direction of the water, his head propped up on his hand.

No way could I discuss *Lolita* with Adam; it's all about this guy who has a thing for young girls. "I just finished *The Sun Also Rises*," I said, changing the subject. "I think it's my new favorite book."

"Yeah," said Adam. "I love that book. The last scene is so great."

"You mean when Brett and Jake are in the taxi?" I said, more than a little amazed to be talking to a boy I liked about a book I liked. "And she says how they could have been so happy together?"

"Exactly," said Adam. "I love when Jake says, 'Isn't it pretty to think so?'"

I was impressed that Adam could quote the actual line. "I love Lady Ashley," I said.

"Really?" asked Adam, craning his neck so he could look at me. "Why?"

120   *Um, because she's irresistible to guys! Because she's beauti-*

ful! Because she's perfect! "She's so independent," is what I settled on. "I admire that."

"I guess," said Adam, sitting up. "She seems kind of sad to me."

"She does?" I was shocked. I mean, yes, Lady Brett *is* sad, what with her true love having died in the war and everything, but Adam was talking about her like he pitied her. How could you pity Lady Brett Ashley? Without thinking about what I was saying, I blurted out, "She's, like, my role model."

I knew Adam was way too nice to suggest I choose a role model who wasn't quite so out of my league, but I never expected him to say what he said next.

"You're way cooler than Lady Brett Ashley."

"Thanks," I said, even though I was having a little trouble breathing.

"You're welcome," he said.

We looked at each other and then we both looked away, and even though we'd been sitting there talking for almost fifteen minutes, I suddenly felt shy.

The silence between us was threatening to grow into something resembling awkward, which wasn't exactly helped by the non sequitur with which I broke it. "It's really beautiful here," I said abruptly.

"You feel like walking?" he asked.

"That would be great," I said, relieved. It's hard to talk when you can't quite catch your breath.

121

Adam stood and took my plate, then walked it over to a garbage can a few feet away before coming back to where I was standing.

We headed away from the party. At first we walked past occasional groups of people, but soon we were heading along a deserted beach. The sky was darker, and I realized Henry had been right—it had gotten cold as the sun went down, and it was all I could do to keep from shivering. I tried, though. Now that we were alone together, far from the madding crowd, the last thing I wanted was for Adam to suggest we turn around and head back so I could go inside and get warm.

By myself.

We'd been walking in silence for a few minutes when Adam said, "Look, you have to let me give you my sweater."

"Aren't you cold?" I asked.

"Yeah," he said. "But I can't possibly be as cold as you are, what with my having a shirt with sleeves and all. And I can't put on my sweater when I'm walking with a girl who's freezing to death."

"I'm not freezing to death," I said, hoping he couldn't hear my teeth chattering.

We'd stopped walking and were facing each other.

"*I'm* freezing to death," he said. "So you must be freezing to death."

"Maybe I'm very warm-blooded," I said.

He untied his sweater from around his waist. "Nobody's that warm-blooded," he said.

"I can't take it," I said. "I'd feel too guilty."

"There's no point in both of us being cold," he said, holding the sweater out to me. "Take the sweater."

"You put it on," I said. "It's your sweater. I'm the one who was stupid enough not to bring one."

"I'm not going to put it on. I can see goose bumps on your flesh." He touched my arm gently, and I shivered, but not just from the cold.

I took a step closer to him.

He'd been holding the sweater bunched up in my direction, but when I stepped toward him, he lifted it up and found the neck. Seeing what he was doing, I took another step and bent my head down. He slipped the sweater over my head, and I felt the soft wool all around me. It smelled of the ocean and the sun, and for a second before my head emerged, I felt myself engulfed in a hot summer's day.

I'd stepped even closer to Adam than I realized; we were only a few inches apart now, and he had his hands on both of my shoulders. I could feel my hair pressing against my ears, pulled tight by the neck of the sweater. I lifted my arms to slip them into the sleeves, and as I pushed my hands down to the cuffs, I extended them toward Adam. Adam reached into the neck of the sweater and gently slipped my hair out, and suddenly it was all too much—his helping me put on the sweater, the two of us alone on the beach. It was like I'd been handed the perfect moment to do something romantic, and before I could think about it, almost before I could decide to do it, my hands were on his hips and I had leaned in to kiss him.

At first he seemed to hesitate about kissing me back, and I got the most horrible sinking feeling in my stomach. I mean, it's one thing to make the first move if you're Lady Brett Ashley and built like a racing yacht and all, but I'm *me*. What if I'd interpreted a gesture of common courtesy as a romantic overture? I could practically hear him talking to Lawrence later. *That Kate girl is so weird. I tried to lend her my sweater and she jumped my bones. It was freaky, man. Do* not *get trapped alone with her.*

But within a second, almost before I had time to think my terrifying humiliating thoughts, Adam's hands were buried in my hair and he was definitely kissing me back.

He was an amazing kisser; that boy Tim, who I'd kissed in Salt Lake, just kind of shoved his tongue in my mouth and left it there, but Adam didn't do anything like that. At first his kisses were really gentle, almost like they were an extension of our flirtatious conversation, and then they got deeper and more intense. When I was kissing Tim I'd found my mind kind of wandering to other things, but kissing Adam was a whole mind-body experience.

I have no idea how long we'd been kissing when the fireworks started going off, but suddenly the world just exploded with light. Adam pulled his lips away from mine and held my face with his hands.

"You're an amazing kisser," he said. "It's just like in the movies—I'm actually seeing fireworks."

I laughed. "Me too."

We both turned and looked out over the water, where the fireworks' dazzle was reflected so it looked like there were two displays—one above the water and one below. Adam slipped his hand into the back pocket of my jeans, and I slipped mine into the back pocket of his. A group of girls who looked like they were about twelve or thirteen walked by, and as they passed, I saw a few of them looking at me and Adam in the light from the fireworks. I realized that they had no idea we'd just kissed for the first time—that to them, we looked like The Perfect Teenage Couple.

And even though *I* knew that we'd just had our first (and for all I knew, *only*) kiss, and we didn't know each other very well, and we lived on opposite sides of the Rocky Mountains, and it was absolutely insane for me to even consider going there . . .

For just a minute, I let myself imagine that we were.

The fireworks finally ended in an explosion of red, white, and blue, which would have been a lot more dramatic and beautiful if they hadn't also ended in a drizzle of rain.

"It would be really awesome if you'd brought a sweater *and* an umbrella."

"If only I were that cool," said Adam.

"No one's that cool," I assured him.

We'd sat down halfway through the fireworks display, and now I stood up and dusted the sand off my butt. Adam stood up too, and we headed back toward the party.

The bonfire was still blazing despite the rain. Because of the drizzle, it seemed to be mostly the under-twenty set who'd remained on the beach, but Jenna, Sarah, and Lawrence weren't among them. We headed up the path toward the golf course. Just as we stepped onto the lawn of the main house, Lawrence appeared.

"We're heading over to Long Nook as soon as it stops raining," he said, mentioning a nearby beach. If he thought it was weird that Adam and I were walking together and that I was wearing Adam's sweater, he didn't say anything.

A crowd was gathering on the porch, but Lawrence knew exactly where to find Jenna and Sarah, who were sitting on the sofa in the library with two guys I'd never seen before and that Victoria girl I'd seen Sarah talking to that first day I came to Larkspur.

"Hey," said Jenna, waving us over.

I wondered if she or Sarah would notice that I was wearing Adam's sweater. I kind of wanted them to notice, wanted them to be like, *What's the deal? Why are you wearing his sweater?* It was like if they noticed the sweater, they were noticing *us* as an *us*. But then I got distracted by the fact that Sarah was wearing a sweater and that Lawrence was sweaterless. Did that mean something had happened with them tonight, too? I remembered what Jenna had said: *He's still into Sarah.* How fun would the rest of the summer be if Sarah and Lawrence became a couple and Adam and I became a couple. (While we were at it, maybe Biff would even come up from wherever he was. It could be the summer of love for everyone!)

As I was imagining the six of us walking along a beach into the sunset, I realized Adam and I had gotten separated by the crowd. For a second I couldn't see him anywhere. Was this a sign that my fantasies were totally insane? (Okay, I knew my fantasies were completely insane, but was this particular separation a sign of that?) Then I looked to my left, and there he was, and I felt my whole body grow warm when he smiled at me through all those people.

A minute later Sarah came over to me. "This is going to be one of those conversations about what to do next that never goes anywhere. Do you want to head home?"

It was really nice how she said it, like maybe if I said I wanted to stay a little while, she'd say okay. Then again, maybe if I said I wanted to stay a little while, she'd say, *Okay then, bye.* Asking Adam for a ride home (did he even have a car?) felt weird and needy. WWLBAD? (What Would Lady Brett Ashley Do?)

"Sure," I said. "Let's head out."

We called good-bye to Adam, Lawrence, and Jenna. Walking away from the porch, I felt cool and fabulous. Maybe Adam would fall madly in love with me. Maybe even after the summer, whenever he hooked up with someone in New York, Jenna would say, *You know, he's madly in love with this girl from Utah. He goes there to ski and see her whenever he can. He even turned down Princeton so he could go to the University of Utah just to be near her.*

Okay, even though none of that was likely to happen, there was consolation in knowing I was guaranteed at least one more conversation with him.

This was waaaay too nice a sweater for him not to ask for it back.

Chapter 12

WHEN I WOKE UP and went outside the next morning, my mom was sitting on the deck of the guesthouse reading a mystery novel and drinking a cup of coffee, her cell phone in her lap. She asked me how the party had been, and I told her it was okay. Then I felt this really, really weird urge to tell her all about Adam. Mostly I think I just wanted to say his name out loud. Luckily, before I had the chance to say something I would have regretted for the rest of the morning (if not my life), she said, "Meg said you and she have been playing phone tag."

"Oh yeah," I said, once again regretting having called my sister.

"She said you sounded extremely distressed in a message you left her," said my mom. "She felt bad that she hadn't reached you."

"No, I'm fine," I said. This was so typical of Meg. Half the time she's saying stuff like, *I wish we could be closer*, the other half she's repeating everything I say to our mother. And I hadn't sounded *extremely distressed*. A little concerned, maybe, but Meg made it sound like I'd been hysterical.

129

"I know this hasn't been easy for you, honey, coming here for the summer. But it's been important for me. I feel so much more centered than I did." I felt bad about my mom thinking I was miserable, especially given the five-star evening I'd just had.

"Don't worry about it, Mom," I said. "Really."

"Well thanks, honey. I know you miss your dad and Laura and everything."

Dad, Laura. Right. It was as if I hadn't thought of either of them in a hundred years.

"Mom, I swear," I said, taking in the sunny day and feeling in it the warmth of Adam's sweater and his arms around me. "I am not mad that we came to Cape Cod, okay?"

She looked at me for a second. "Okay," she said. "I'll take you at your word."

"Good," I said. "I'm going to get some breakfast. I have to teach a lesson this morning."

"Are you feeling more optimistic about it than you were the other night?" she asked.

"Mostly I'm feeling like instead of giving Natasha a lesson, I should just take a hit out on her dad." I slipped a ponytail holder around my hair.

"You and your dad are so close," said my mom. "Maybe you could help her be closer to her dad."

Was it my imagination, or did my mom seem sad when she said my dad and I were close? It made me feel a tiny bit guilty, like I should say something to make her feel better. But what? *We're not that close? You and I are close too?* But neither of those things was true. I could have said, *Well, you and Meg are really close*, but that seemed nasty, as if I were implying she could only be close to one of her daughters and she'd made her choice.

I ended up just saying, "Yeah, maybe," which sounded really lame.

My mom's phone rang, and she looked to see who was calling. "I should take this," she said. Then she added, "Remember, reach out to Natasha. Get to know her," before saying, "Hello!" in this really cheerful voice.

I wondered if it was my dad who'd called, and as I walked up to the house I realized that if they reconciled, it might mean I'd have to leave Cape Cod sooner rather than later. If we went back to Salt Lake, would I be able to go back to Ms. Baker's class? It would be cool to keep working on my story about the little boy, if I could show it to her. Then again, if we left now, what would happen with me and Adam? Thinking about kissing him made it hard to get excited about having my work critiqued by even the most insightful reader. . . .

I would have said I was feeling so benevolent toward the universe that nothing could upset my perfect equilibrium, but apparently this was not the case. Mr. Davis's behavior, it seemed, had the power to disturb even the world's most balanced soul. Each time he critiqued Natasha's stroke (that is to say, each time she lifted her racket), I could practically hear my blood pressure rising. It didn't help that I was pretty sure he was holding himself back from commenting on *my* playing. Here I was, sixteen years old, about to be a junior in high school, a reasonably accomplished tennis player (if I do say so myself), with more than a few trophies on my bedroom shelf, and this guy made me worried about my ability to make contact with the ball. It was enough to make *me* want to quit playing, and I wasn't even his daughter.

Why did it not surprise me when his cell phone ringer played "Hail to the Chief"?

"Jim Davis," he shouted into it. (Did the man ever not shout?) "What? What? I'm having trouble hearing you." As if to overcompensate for the difficulty he was having hearing his caller, Mr. Davis raised his voice until it seemed he could have communicated with anyone anywhere in the world even without the help of the cell phone in his hand.

Just as I was sure a player on one of the adjoining courts was going to start complaining, Mr. Davis snapped his phone shut in disgust.

"Honey, I have to go see what the hell's going on at the office," he said. "Will you be okay if I leave?"

It was all I could do to keep a straight face. Luckily,

he was looking at his daughter, not me. "I think I can handle it," she said.

"Meet me at the clubhouse when you're done, okay?"

"Yup," she said. Natasha watched her dad as he made his way up the steps to the wide lawn separating the tennis courts from the clubhouse. Then she turned back to face me. I was about to hit a ball to her when I thought about what my mom had said.

"Want to take a little break?" I asked.

"What?" she asked, but I had the feeling she'd heard me.

"I said, do you want to take a little break? Talk for a minute?" It occurred to me that she might think I was trying to get out of teaching her now that her dad wasn't around to keep an eye on me; but since the question was out of my mouth (and not once, but twice), I couldn't exactly say, *Just kidding, let's play some tennis.*

She looked at me for a long beat. "Okay," she said.

We headed over to the bench where her dad had been sitting. Then we just sat there, neither of us saying anything.

"So, um . . . your dad seems to be really into your playing tennis."

Natasha snorted. "You think?"

"My dad was the same way," I said, relieved to have such an easy opening. Again, I remembered my mom's advice. "He was sort of like my coach for a while. Before 133

I started playing on the team in high school."

"Yes," said Natasha, "but you like tennis."

She had a point. "And I'm guessing you don't?"

"Bingo!"

Maybe this was stating the obvious, but I couldn't resist. "So, um, do you ever think about not playing?"

"Let's just say that isn't really an option where my dad is concerned."

But you don't have to play if you don't want to. I almost uttered the sentence, but then I considered my mom dragging me to Cape Cod. Who was I to not understand that sometimes we are powerless in the face of parental demands?

"Okay," I said. We appeared to have hit a dead end, since the only thing I could think of to say was, *I'm really sorry that your dad is such a total ass*, which maybe wasn't the kind of thing you're supposed to say to a minor you're supposedly educating. I decided to make a U-turn and try to find another route to closeness. "Do you come up to Cape Cod every summer?"

"Pretty much," she said. Then she didn't say anything else.

"And do you like it?" I remembered Adam asking me the same question last night. Thinking of him made me feel so jittery I almost suggested to Natasha that we run a few laps.

"It's okay," said Natasha without enthusiasm. Clearly

she had not read the advice of the creators of the "Are You a Good-Time Girl?" quiz.

"Tina said you're from New York. Do you have friends up here?"

"I guess," she said. "Some."

When my mother recommended talking to your students about something other than the subject you were teaching, had she, in fact, been able to *reach* her students, or was she just speaking theoretically? Because if she'd had success with kids like Natasha, she shouldn't go back to teaching. . . .

She should negotiate a peace settlement in the Middle East.

I racked my brain for another question. The women on the next court were gathering up their things, and people were heading down from the pro shop to the courts, which meant it must have been almost eleven.

"Um, are you—"

Luckily she cut me off before it became clear that I didn't have an actual question prepared.

"Well, I should go," she said. "I think the hour is up."

"Oh, really?" Was my fake surprise even remotely believable? I highly doubted it.

A bunch of guys headed down the steps. I half noticed two of them peel away from the group and head toward the court Natasha and I had been playing on.

"Hey, Kate," called one of them, and I saw that it was Adam and Lawrence.

Every thought I'd had about Adam all morning had been a good one, but now that I was actually seeing him, I started to feel a little nervous. How were we going to greet each other? Should I just be all, *Hey, dudes*, like it was no different seeing Adam than it was seeing Lawrence?

My hands were actually shaking. It was a good thing I wasn't trying to hit a tennis ball at this particular moment.

Lawrence stopped at the edge of the court and unzipped his warm-up jacket, but Adam came over to the bench where Natasha and I were sitting.

"Hey," he said. He reached out and tapped my shoulder gently with his racket.

"Hey," I said. Even my *voice* was shaking. I hoped Natasha and Adam didn't know me well enough to notice.

"You ladies want to watch us play?" asked Lawrence. He dropped his bag, took out his racket, and unzipped the cover. "A lot of girls would kill to have the opportunity."

"I'm gonna go," said Natasha, standing up. "Bye, Kate."

"Okay," I said, glad that my voice sounded a little stronger.

"I guess my mom will call about another lesson," she said. Then she reached into her pocket and took out a crinkled twenty dollar bill. "Here," she said.

I was so discombobulated I would never have remembered to get money from Natasha if she hadn't offered it. "Thanks," I said. "You know, if you don't want to have any more lessons—"

"Don't worry about it," she said. "This is way bigger than you."

I knew I should take her comment as an opportunity to get her to open up to me, but now clearly wasn't the time for me to have an actual conversation with anyone. What I needed was to go soak my head in a bucket of ice water.

When Natasha had headed down the path to the stairs, Adam said, "You extorting money from the twelve-and-under set?" he asked.

"Basically," I said. It felt okay to be talking to him now, by which I mean I could form thoughts and words. "That's the girl I'm supposedly teaching how to play tennis."

"I'm intrigued. How do you 'supposedly' teach tennis to someone?"

Lawrence took out a can of tennis balls from his bag, popped it open, and slipped one of the balls into each of his pockets, then bounced the third against his racket two or three times experimentally. "You coming to The Clam Shack later, Kate?" he asked.

"The Clam Shack?" I asked.

"Great seafood, crap music," he said, crossing to the other side of the court, still bouncing the tennis ball.

Would Adam have asked me to go out with them if Lawrence hadn't? Was Lawrence asking *for* Adam? It was the kind of thing I could imagine two girls arranging, but not two guys.

"Yeah, will I see you later?" asked Adam. The way he said it made me pretty sure he wanted to see me later.

"Great seafood, crap music," I said. "Who could argue with that?"

"Not to mention the company," said Adam, and he smiled at me in a way that I knew had to do with our kiss last night.

"Not to mention the company," I repeated, smiling back at him the same way.

"Adam Carpenter, you are a dead man," called Lawrence. "These delaying tactics are but a pathetic attempt to avoid the inevitable." Out of the corner of my eye I saw Lawrence pick up a ball between his foot and racket.

"I guess I'll see you later," I said.

"Later," Adam said.

We didn't kiss or even touch or anything, but as I made my way off the court and up the lawn to the club-house, I felt as tingly as if we had.

Despite our having left the party together last night, I wasn't sure how to tell Sarah about my invitation to The Clam Shack, but when I got home, she was sitting in the kitchen eating a sandwich, and even before I could say anything, she said, "I'm about to go to work, but do you want to get dinner at The Clam Shack tonight with everyone? I'll be home in time to drive you."

"Yeah, sure," I said. "Great." I hoped I'd earned Sarah's invitation, that it had more to do with my having not made a fool of myself at the barbecue than with what her dad had said to her the other night when they were putting out the garbage. It seemed like a legitimate invitation, what with her asking me so nicely despite neither of her parents being within earshot. And from what I'd overheard, Henry had only forced her to invite me to the Fourth of July party, not to every single social event of the summer.

Seven o'clock found me sitting in the passenger seat of her car as we cruised along Route 6. Sarah had cranked the music to an ear-splitting volume again, but I tried not to analyze it. Maybe she was avoiding talking to me, maybe she just liked listening to The Lowdowners really loud.

Whatever.

The Clam Shack was a tiny wooden . . . well, shack, just off Route 6. Inside was a small stage and a bar, half a dozen tables, and about the same number of booths, at one of which Jenna, Lawrence, and Adam were already sitting when Sarah and I got there. We slid onto the empty bench, and I was glad it worked out that I was directly across from Adam.

Right before getting in the car with Sarah, I'd tried to decide what to do about returning his sweater. I considered wearing it to The Clam Shack, but that seemed presumptuous, like I assumed he'd given it to me or something. Then I was going to carry it so I could just walk in and give it to him, but at the last second I decided to leave it on my bed. Even though he'd seemed psyched to see me on the tennis court, if our kiss had just been a random one-time thing, the last thing I wanted was to remind him about it in front of everyone by handing over the sweater. If he made it clear that he wasn't into me, surely there'd be some point over the next few weeks when I could subtly return it to him in a way that didn't announce *I'm the total loser who jumped*

Adam's bones on the Fourth of July. I strongly suggest that each of you think long and hard the next time you have the urge to make a chivalrous gesture to a shivering stranger.

We'd all barely said hello when the waitress came over to take our orders. There weren't any menus, but everyone ordered a lobster, so I did too, glad about the lessons I'd been giving Natasha when I saw the prices chalked on the wall. Almost as soon as we'd ordered, a guy with shaggy hair and a guitar stepped up onstage and said, "Check one. Check two," into the microphone, then strummed a few chords on his guitar before saying, "Could I have a little more vocals?" to someone at the back of the room.

The lights dimmed and a spotlight came up on the guy, who started singing a folksy tune I didn't know and definitely didn't like. His voice was sort of thin, and he kept playing the same chord over and over again. I thought the lobsters were going to have to be seriously great to make up for what a lousy performer we were listening to, but then Adam slipped his foot in between mine, and we made eye contact across the table, and I realized I didn't actually care what the food tasted like.

"I'm thinking Maine," said Lawrence. "Because that way if we want to be wimps, we can always crash at your grandparents."

"Maine works for me," said Adam, expertly cracking a lobster claw open.

Clearly everyone at the table other than me had been born with a nutcracker in one hand and a lobster in the other, because they were all managing to do the impossible, which was get a meal out of the huge red bug on their plates. I, meanwhile, was more hungry than I'd been when I sat down, no doubt because of all the calories I'd burned trying to break into the vault that was my lobster.

"What's in Maine?" I asked, trying to smile as I worked to sever the lobster's tail from its body.

"Fishing," said Lawrence. "Awesome fly fishing."

"Adam and Lawrence do this annual fishing trip," explained Jenna. "They go off into the wilderness for three days. It's hugely—"

"Macho," finished Lawrence.

"I was going to say 'gay,'" said Jenna. "But you should believe whatever you need to."

"Is David going to be back in time or what?" asked Lawrence, dipping a piece of lobster into Sarah's butter. I was so hungry I had to look away from the delicious bite he thrust into his mouth.

"I think so," said Adam. "He's back from Colorado next week."

"He is?" asked Sarah.

"Who's David?" I asked. Was I being annoying? This was the second question I'd asked in as many minutes. Normally I just like to go with the flow when people are

discussing things I don't know about, but when it came

to Adam, I found myself wanting to understand stuff I wouldn't usually care about.

"My brother," said Adam. "He's on a NOLS thing in Colorado."

"You have a brother?" I was really surprised. I couldn't believe I'd fooled around with someone I didn't know had a brother. Not that it mattered or anything, but I'd been putting together this picture of Adam, and now I had to insert a brother where there hadn't been one before.

"We're twins, actually," he said.

Now it felt really weird that I hadn't known about David. I mean, a random brother was one thing— someone with Adam's actual DNA was another. "Identical?" I asked.

Lawrence, Sarah, and Jenna laughed.

"Maybe from the back," said Jenna.

"In the dark," said Sarah.

"To a blind person," added Lawrence.

Adam shook his head, laughing too. I wondered if David was some kind of uber geek or something. "In answer to your question, no, we're fraternal twins."

"But you know what's weird?" said Jenna. "You guys have the same voice. I can never tell if it's you or David when I call your house."

"Really?" asked Sarah. "I can always tell."

I was still trying to integrate this latest deposit to my

savings account of Adam-related information when Jenna said, "We should go somewhere too. What's the female equivalent of a fishing trip?"

"Spa," said Sarah.

"You're such a feminist," I said, laughing. I don't know if I would have had the confidence to make a joke at Sarah's expense if I hadn't had my feet twisted up with Adam's under the table.

"The whole 'what should we do while the guys are away' thing isn't exactly a feminist paradigm, is it?" Sarah pointed out.

"Touché," said Lawrence. By then we were all laughing, even Sarah, so I wasn't worried I'd said the wrong thing.

"Oh, you know what? We should go whale watching!" said Jenna excitedly. "We haven't gone yet this summer."

"For three days?" asked Sarah.

"No, no, not while the guys are fishing," said Jenna. "All of us. Soon. Saturday."

I was glad she turned to me then (would there ever come a time again when I just assumed "we" included me?) and asked, "Have you ever been whale watching?"

"Nope," I said. I didn't add that I'd spent last summer reading *Moby Dick*, and that the idea of spending any amount of time, be it three days or three hours, on a boat chasing a whale sounded to me about as sensible as going smallpox hunting.

"See!" said Jenna, practically jumping up and down in her chair, "Kate's never gone whale watching. We have to go. It's a once-in-a-lifetime experience, Kate."

"So why are those of us who have already gone going again?" asked Sarah.

"Because, one, we cannot deny Kate the opportunity to have a once-in-a-lifetime experience," said Lawrence. "And two, we're total losers with nothing else to do."

"Hey!" said Sarah. "Speak for yourself." She reached across the table and pushed at his shoulder. Maybe I was imagining things, but it seemed to me that Lawrence blushed a little when she touched him.

"So, okay, Saturday. Whale watching," said Jenna.

"Sure," said Sarah.

"Most definitely," said Lawrence.

"I'm in," said Adam.

"Me too," I said. The truth was, I didn't really care about whales. It was a day spent playing footsie with Adam that sounded like my idea of a once-in-a-lifetime experience.

When Jenna suggested we all go for a walk on the beach after dinner, part of me really wanted to say yes. What could be more romantic than a walk on the beach with the guy you made out with just last night and desperately wanted to make out with again? But then I was like, what if he just walks ahead with Lawrence? What if we can kiss and play footsie, but only if no one knows about what's going on with us? And then I was like, what *is* going on with us, anyway?

"I'll go," said Lawrence.

If the two of us were on the beach together and he didn't take my hand or kiss me or anything, I was going to feel like *such* an idiot.

Better safe than sorry.

"Actually," I said, "I'm kind of beat."

And then, as if we were speaking some kind of secret code that nobody but we could understand, Adam said, "I'm beat too. I can bring Kate home."

I can bring Kate home. Suddenly these were my five favorite words in the English language.

"Thanks," said Sarah.

"It's stupid to bring three cars to the beach," said Jenna. "Why don't I drive and then I'll bring you guys back here to pick your cars up."

"You're so environmentally savvy," said Lawrence.

"She is," said Sarah. "Jenna of the tiny carbon footprint. Oh, and Lawrence?"

"Yeah?"

"Shotgun."

"You bitch!" said Lawrence, laughing. "You do this to me every time."

As we said our good-byes and I followed Adam over to his car, my stomach was jumpy enough for me to be
146   glad I'd barely gotten half a dozen bites of lobster.

"Aah, the ubiquitous Subaru wagon," I said, sliding into the seat just as my cell rang. "You don't see too many of these around." It was my dad calling, so I just hit IGNORE. Here's who you don't want to talk to when you're driving alone with a guy you like: your dad.

When an opening in the traffic appeared, Adam gunned the engine to make the left onto Route 6. Over the course of my visit I'd learned this was just how people on Cape Cod drove, and I no longer clutched the sides of my seat and held my breath when it happened.

"Wow," I said, checking out the sky through the windshield. "Look at the stars. I mean, not now," I added quickly, what with his driving and all.

"I figured," he said, reaching for my hand. He twined his fingers through mine, and we drove, neither of us saying anything.

When we pulled into Sarah's driveway, both the main house and the guesthouse were dark. I decided to assume my mom and Tina were at a movie together and Jamie and Henry were at the driving range or out for dinner, rather than some alternative combination, e.g., my mom and Jamie at a movie together. After all, why borrow trouble?

Adam shut the car off, and I turned to face him. "Thanks for the ride," I said.

"Glad I could be of help," he said.

I thought Adam was about to lean forward and kiss 147

me, but instead he reached out with his hand and carefully traced my lips. It felt really nice, like a cross between sexy and friendly. Then he moved his hand to the back of my neck and gently pulled me toward him. For a second I worried that he might be thinking I was a lame kisser, but then I had my hands in his hair, and I was too busy kissing him back to worry about anything.

"Wow," he said when we finally came up for air. He leaned his forehead against mine. We were both breathing kind of fast.

"Yeah," I said. "Wow."

"I had a great time tonight," I said.

"Me too," he said. He kissed me again. "I can't stop kissing you." Apparently I couldn't stop kissing him either because that's what we sat there doing until we heard the crackle of a car pulling into the gravel behind us. We separated just as Tina's car pulled up next to ours; even the fact that only she and Henry, not my mother or Jamie, got out couldn't dim my happiness.

Adam rolled down his window, breaking the spell.

"Hi, Tina," he called. "Hi, Henry."

"Is that Adam?" said Tina. She came over and poked her head in. "Hi, guys."

"Hi," I said.

Henry came and stood next to the car. "You want to come in for some hot chocolate?" he asked. "It's cold out."

Adam shook his head. "No thanks," he said. "I've got to get home. Sarah should be here soon. They went to check out the beach."

"Okay," said Tina. "Well, good night."

They headed inside, arms around each other's waists.

Adam turned to me, and we started making out again, but I was a little nervous that my mom would pull up behind us any second. Even if she didn't actually catch us, she'd be sure to wonder why we were sitting in the car.

"I should go," I said. Our lips were still touching, so it came out kind of muffled.

"Don't go," said Adam, kissing me again. "Wait, what are you doing tomorrow?"

"Tomorrow?" I asked. It was like I wasn't sure what the word meant. "Um . . . I don't know. I don't have any plans."

"Do you want to go to Provincetown?" He was kissing the side of my neck. It was extraordinarily hard to focus on what he was saying.

"What?" I said.

He kissed his way up to my ear, then whispered, "Do you want to go to Provincetown with me tomorrow?"

His lips tickled against my earlobe, and I giggled, not just because of the tickling but because I couldn't believe he'd just asked me to spend the day with him. Me. Kate Draper! "Really?" I said.

"No, I'm joking," he said. "Yes, really." And then we kissed again.

"Okay," I said.

"Okay," he said. Our foreheads were pressed together and we were both smiling. "I'll pick you up at ten o'clock."

"Wait a minute," I said. "Don't you have to work?"

"Not until the afternoon. I'm yours until four."

I liked the idea of Adam being mine.

"So I guess I'll see you at ten," I said.

"I guess so," he said. I pulled myself away from him and undid my seat belt, then stepped out of the car. As soon as I did, Adam rolled down my window.

"Hey," he called.

I leaned into the car.

"You're awesome, you know that?" he said.

"Am I?" I asked. I didn't mean to sound coy, it was just so . . . crazy. The whole thing. I mean, no guy had ever told me I was awesome. Over the years guys had told me I was nice. And smart. And funny. But awesome? Awesome like, *I love kissing you* awesome?

Not so much.

"Yes, Kate," he said. "You are awesome."

I winked at him and turned away, heading toward the house. I didn't know if it was Adam's saying it or just an accumulation of the night's overall perfection, but the fact was, I'd never felt so awesome in my entire life.

Chapter 14

THE WHOLE IDEA of the musical has always confused me. I mean, how is it realistic that a person would suddenly break into song for no reason, like, *Hello! I am so excited to be on the train now.* But honestly, all morning that's exactly what I felt like doing. *I am eating my breakfast on this beautiful day! Has there ever been such a beautiful day? Hooray! Hooray!* Sarah had already left for the historical society, and I was sitting on the back deck, with my mom and Henry and Tina and Jamie when I heard Adam's car pull into the driveway. I was in such a good mood I hadn't even been irritated with Jamie when he'd refilled my mom's coffee cup earlier.

I stood up. "I should go," I said.

My mom looked up from reading her paper. "Where are you going?" she asked. "Do you want a ride?"

"No, my ride's here. I mean, my friend's here. I'm going to Provincetown with my friend today." I purposely left out any gender-identifying pronoun. I didn't think my mom would suddenly freak out about my   151 spending the day with a guy she didn't know, but you can never be too sure.

"Sounds like fun," said Jamie.

I heard a car door shut. I had Adam's sweater and my bag by the front door so I wouldn't have to keep him waiting.

"Enjoy," said my mom.

I couldn't believe it. I wasn't going to get a whole cross-examination from my mom about who I was going with and what time I'd be home and had the person had his/her driver's license for at least thirty years.

It was almost too good to be true.

"Thanks," I said. "You too."

"Have a great time," said Henry. "Are you going with Jenna?"

Damn! So close. "Oh," I said. "No, actually. I'm going with Adam." Saying his name felt so nice. Adam. Adam. *AdamAdamAdam.*

For a second everything seemed to freeze. The screen door to the front of the house opened and then slammed shut.

"Kate?" called Adam.

Was my mom going to throw a hissy fit?

"I'll be right there," I called. Then I held my breath for a count of three.

But all that happened was Adam appeared. "Hey," I said.

"Hey," he said, spotting me through the screen door. He came out to the deck, then said hello to Tina and Henry.

"This is my brother, Jamie," said Tina. Jamie stood up, and he and Adam shook hands.

There was a pause, and then my mom said, "And I'm Jane, Kate's mom."

Oh my God, how incredibly lame am I?! "I'm so sorry," I said quickly. "Adam, this is my mom. Mom, this is my"—I hesitated, but I don't think anyone else noticed—"friend Adam." Were we friends? I mean, we didn't actually know each other all that well. Then again, we'd had our tongues in each other's mouths. So in some ways we knew each other very well.

Honestly, the whole thing was so confusing it was enough to make you wish you lived in a Jane Austen novel, where you practically couldn't even go for a *walk* alone with a guy unless you were engaged to him.

"Hi, Adam," said my mom. "It's nice to meet you."

"Hi," said Adam. "It's nice to meet you too."

"Well, I guess we should go." I said it kind of abruptly, but I couldn't just stand there with everyone making small talk. Nobody else seemed to find the scene playing out on the deck awkward, but I was nervous enough to wish I were wearing one of those special deodorants that promises to *never let them see you sweat.*

"Sure." My mom smiled at me in this really

understanding way, like she knew I was kind of freaking out. I made a pact with myself that I wouldn't say anything mean to her for at least twenty-four hours. "Have a great time."

As Adam and I sat at a red light on Route 6, I tried to figure out what had made me feel so weird when he was saying hello to everyone. The thing was, I'd never had a boy meet my parents before. I mean, a quick hello to my mom wasn't like *meeting the parents* in some kind of big significant way; but still.

"Your mom seems nice," said Adam.

"Thanks," I said, and I was so relieved that I actually giggled a little. Then the light changed and he hit the gas and we were on our way.

Provincetown was founded in 1727, which, when you think about it, was a long, long time ago. As we walked the tiny streets, I couldn't believe how many houses were squeezed together in such a small space or how beautifully they were designed and decorated, with elaborate flower gardens on plots the size of postage stamps, and bright multicolored porches sporting rainbow flags.

"I love all the rainbows," I said. "They're so colorful." We were walking along Commercial Street, people watching. There were families eating ice cream and 154 women dressed in outlandish dresses handing out flyers for nighttime shows, and lots and lots of young guys in great shape. A few were so muscular I wondered if there was some kind of Olympic tryout being held nearby.

"I like the rainbows too," he said. "They're a good symbol."

"Yeah," I said, too engrossed in everything to really register what he'd said. A second later, when his words sank in, I asked, "Wait, symbol of what?"

Adam stopped walking and turned to face me. "Are you serious?" he asked.

I racked my brain. Pink ribbon—breast cancer. Yellow ribbon—remember our troops. The letter P with a line through it—no parking.

"I'm serious," I said. "Give me a hint."

He thought for a second. "Okay," he said, "'Somewhere Over the Rainbow.'"

"*The Wizard of Oz*!" I shouted, glad I'd gotten it on the first try. Then I looked around. "The rainbow is the symbol of *The Wizard of Oz*?"

Adam started laughing. Seriously laughing. Like, hysterically. A few times he tried to stop, but then he'd start again. He was laughing so hard he could barely squeak out the words, "Friends of Dorothy."

Adam's laughter was contagious, but I still had no idea what he was talking about. "Who is Dorothy?" I asked. "Do you mean Dorothy Gale? From *The Wizard of Oz*?"

"Is that her last name?" asked Adam, who'd finally calmed down enough to speak. "Gale?"

"Yes," I said. "But why are these people friends of hers?"

You could tell Adam wanted to start laughing again, but he restrained himself. "The rainbow is a symbol of homosexuality. Like, it means a place is friendly to gay people or that it supports a gay lifestyle. It comes from *The Wizard of Oz*—the idea of being happy somewhere else. You know—"

"Somewhere over the rainbow," I finished, feeling like the biggest hick on the planet. So it wasn't that there just happened to be a lot of hot guys running around without their wives or girlfriends in Provincetown. There were a lot of *gay* guys in Provincetown.

"Right," he said. "Somewhere over the rainbow. Also, Judy Garland is kind of big in gay culture, but I'm not exactly sure why."

"Wow," I said. "You must think I'm about as sophisticated as a Big Mac."

He draped his arm around me. "Don't sweat it," he said. "I imagine you don't have a lot of rainbows in Salt Lake City."

"Not so many," I said.

We walked along for a few minutes before he said, "Weren't all the transvestites we passed kind of a clue?"

"What transvestites?" I asked.

"Oh my God," he said, squeezing me to him and kissing the top of my head. "We'd better get some lunch."

Halfway through lunch at a bistro overlooking the water, Adam's cell rang.

"Hey, Lawrence," he said, picking it up.

While he talked, I looked around the restaurant so it wouldn't seem as if I were eavesdropping on his conversation. After what Adam had told me, it was pretty obvious that there were a lot of gay men in Provincetown. Sitting at a restaurant where at least half of the tables were populated by all male groups or couples made me feel kind of cool. I felt like going up to them and saying, *You know, this is my first meal in a gay restaurant in a gay town. I'm from Salt Lake City.* Obviously I didn't, but being in a place that was so casual about gay people just added to the excitement of being with Adam. It was like he hadn't just taken me to a new town, he'd taken me to a new planet.

"Sure, man, I understand. Don't worry about it. . . . You know, if I can swap some days off with one of the other interns, I can do it. . . . So coming back Wednesday or . . . Yeah, let me just ask around. . . . No, I'm in P-town, I'm working later. . . . Yeah, I'll call you when I know. . . . Okay, sure. . . . Great."

Was it weird that he hadn't said he was in P-town with me? Or would it have been weird if he *had* said he was here with me? Between my not knowing what to call Adam and forgetting to introduce him to my mom and being worried that he didn't tell Lawrence he was having lunch with me, I was starting to feel in need of a Web site called firsttimedaters.com. Or maybe instead of writing a novel, I could write something like, "Your First Relationship: When it Starts, What it's Called, How to Deal."

If other girls out there were even half as clueless as I was, the book was sure to be a best seller.

"So," said Adam, flipping his phone shut. "What do you want first, the good news or the bad news?"

"Um, the bad news."

"Okay, Lawrence has a family reunion thing the weekend we were supposed to go fishing, so we're going to try and go tomorrow. Which means we can't go whale watching with you guys."

Was that all? I was a little sad not to get to go whale watching with Adam, but I'd been afraid he was going to say something like, *Lawrence needs a heart transplant, so I'm going from lunch directly to the Mayo Clinic in Minnesota for the rest of the summer. But it was nice knowing you.*

I could live with a three-day fishing trip.

"Bummer," I said.

He smiled at my mellow response. "You *are* cool," he said.

"Thanks," I said. *Cool. Awesome.* If those weren't Lady

Brett Ashley adjectives, I didn't know what were. "Now, what's the good news?"

He reached across the table and took my hand. "The good news," he said, "is that we're less than a hundred yards from the best ice cream on God's green earth, and I'm about to buy you a cone."

I leaned toward him. "That *is* good news," I said.

And, like I'd known he would, he met me halfway with a kiss.

The ice cream was pretty amazing, but it wasn't as amazing as the used bookstore, where we ended the afternoon. There must have been ten thousand books piled everywhere, the system of organization vague enough that Adam assured me I shouldn't even try to find something specific. "Just let yourself get lost," he said, which is exactly what I did. I was sitting on a pile of books, reading a novel about a crazy apartment building in San Francisco where all of the people know each other and the landlady is more or less the tenants' mom, when Adam tapped me on the shoulder. He was holding a book in his hand, but I couldn't read the title.

"I'm just going to pay for this," he said. "I'll meet you outside."

"Sure," I said, starting to stand up.

"Take your time," he said, putting his hand on my shoulder. "I'll be on the porch."

Even though he'd said he didn't mind, I felt weird sitting and reading while Adam waited for me, so I just finished the page I was on and decided I'd buy the book, which cost only a dollar. As I was walking up to the cash register, I passed a slightly shabby paperback copy of *The Wizard of Oz*. Without letting myself stop and think about it, I took it off the shelf. Then I paid for both and went outside. Adam looked up at the tinkling bell of the screen door.

"Hey," he said.

"Hey," I said. I held the book out for him. "I figured since you didn't know her last name, maybe you'd never read the book."

"Oh, this is great," he said, taking it from me. "I've seen the movie, but you're right, I never read it." He was smiling, and I could tell he really was glad about my getting him the book. "Thanks."

"You're welcome," I said.

Then he reached into the paper bag he'd had on his lap and pulled out an equally tattered paperback. "This is for you. You said you like *The Sun Also Rises*. This is supposed to be Hemingway's nonfiction account of the time he spent in Paris."

The book was called *A Moveable Feast*, and the cover had a line drawing of a window looking out over the Parisian skyline.

"Oh, wow," I said. "Thank you so much. I've never 160 even heard of this book."

"Kind of like the rainbows," he said.

I hit him in the head with my gift. "Watch yourself, Carpenter," I said. "I like you and all, but really."

"So," he said, raising one eyebrow at me, "you like me, do you?"

For a second everything got really still. "Maybe I do," I said.

"Hunh," he said. "Well, maybe I like you too." We stood there looking at each other, letting what we'd said sink in a little. Then he took my hand and we walked down the street and headed to the car.

Chapter 15

"THE GUYS BAILED," said Jenna around a mouthful of toast. "But we don't care." She gestured to the plate of toast in front of her. "Have one."

It was a little before nine on Saturday, and I'd come up to the main house to find Jenna and Sarah eating breakfast on the deck. In the kitchen my mom and Tina and Henry and Jamie were talking about what they kept referring to as "the political scene" in New York. I could understand Tina and Henry and Jamie caring about it, since it had become extremely clear to me that New Yorkers never tired of talking, thinking, or hearing about New York, but my mom's interest in the subject escaped me. Usually all my mom wanted to talk about was whether or not it was time to redecorate the downstairs bathroom.

"Yeah," said Sarah. "The siren song of male bonding was just too powerful to resist, so Adam and Lawrence left on their fishing trip this morning."

I wasn't sure what to say. *I know?* Then they'd want to

know how I knew, and I'd have to say, *Well, Adam and I are kind of . . . what? Kind of going out?* Could you *be* kind of going out, or was going out something you were or you weren't? And no one had said anything about going out. It wasn't like Adam had said, *Will you go out with me?* But did people even say that anymore? Was that an anachronism along the lines of going to the soda shop for a pop and having a boy carry your books home from school and getting pinned?

But you *know* if you're going out with someone. Like, Laura was clearly going out with Brad. As far as I knew, she still had his sweatshirt. I, on the other hand, had felt obligated to return Adam's sweater yesterday. Question: Were he my boyfriend, would I have kept the sweater?

"Would you?"

I realized that Jenna and Sarah were both looking at me and that there had been silence for a second or two. Since they weren't mind readers, they must have asked about something other than Adam's sweater.

"Sorry," I said. "What?"

"Would you describe yourself as someone who gets seasick?" asked Jenna.

"Not that I know of," I said. Though, considering I'd never actually been on the sea, I probably didn't *not* get seasick so much as I'd never had the opportunity to *get* seasick.

"Oh, you're lucky. I get soo sick. It's the worst." 163

"But you're the one who wanted to go on the whale watch," I pointed out.

Jenna wrinkled her nose. "I know," she said. "But I'm planning on being a marine biologist, so I've got to get used to it."

I had to put Adam out of my mind or I was going to drive myself insane. He liked me. He'd *said* he liked me. And then when we'd kissed good-bye, he'd given me a really tight squeeze and said, *I'll be fishing with Lawrence, but I'll be thinking about you.*

If that wasn't practically as good as asking someone out, I didn't know what was. It was time to focus on something else.

"I don't know anything about marine biology," I said. I took a piece of toast from the pile and sliced a piece of cheddar cheese to put on it.

"Oh, you will," said Sarah, spreading cream cheese on her own piece of toast. "When you're on the water with Jenna, you learn a lot about marine biology."

I was glad to see that even with Jenna in the car, Sarah blasted music—apparently it wasn't simply her desire to avoid conversation with me that had her playing her favorite artists at top volume. We didn't talk much on the way to Provincetown, but at one point, when we'd been driving for about fifteen minutes, Sarah reached over and lowered the volume.

"You know, if you say the word humpback enough, it doesn't even sound dirty," she said. "Try it."

"Humpback," said Jenna, and she immediately cracked up.

"Humpback," I said. It was impossible to say the word without laughing.

Sarah was smiling. "Hmm," she said, reaching for the volume knob again. "Guess I was wrong."

The *Queequeg* was a much smaller boat than I'd anticipated—I'd been picturing something along the lines of a Princess Cruises ship, a kind of floating condominium that couldn't possibly capsize no matter how enormous the sea life it encountered might prove to be. The tickets were way more expensive than I'd been anticipating, too. Between whales and lobsters, I'd run through Mr. Davis's money and started digging into my own.

Jenna brought us upstairs to the open-air deck even though she said we wouldn't be seeing any whales for a while. As we pulled away from the dock, I could see why she'd wanted to stay outside—it was an incredible feeling, the spray on my face, the slight *bump bump bump* as the boat skimmed over the water on its way out to sea. I felt a tingle of anxiety in the pit of my stomach even though I didn't think I was especially nervous about seeing whales or even about the boat tipping over. Still, with the speed and the air and the sunlight on the water, it felt like something exciting or unexpected or even dangerous was about to happen.

When the coastline was nothing but a dark smudge in the distance, I turned to Jenna. "It's like a movie," I said. "Or a music video." We were flying along now, and leaning against the rail with the wind blowing my hair and the sun in my face, I felt very glamorous.

"You look like Jackie O," said Jenna.

"Totally," said Sarah.

For no reason I felt like laughing. Between my day with Adam and feeling like Sarah and Jenna were really my friends . . . It was all so amazing I didn't even care if we saw any whales.

"If you'll look over to the port, or left, side of the boat," said a voice over the loudspeaker, "you'll see—"

"Look!" yelled Jenna, pointing out toward the horizon. "Whales!"

I followed her finger. Maybe two hundred yards away was a group of what I guess were whales. One was much larger than the others, which were small enough that they looked like nothing more than small lumps.

I couldn't help feeling a little disappointed. They were just . . . bumps in the ocean. People around us *Ooh*ed and *Aah*ed as they directed their cameras toward the sight, but I couldn't see what was so special. I didn't want to be a bad sport, though, so I opened my eyes wide, hoping I looked like someone who was amazed by what she was seeing.

As we watched, the largest bump disappeared and immediately pushed high up out of the water. I gasped as water sprayed off its gigantic body; it seemed to hover in the air for an impossibly long time before it dipped below the water, its tail still waving against the horizon.

"Oh my God," I said, barely aware of having said it. I wasn't faking my look of amazement anymore.

Jenna was standing next to me, and she bumped my shoulder with hers. "I know," she said quietly. "Isn't it incredible?"

I'd honestly never seen anything like it in my life. No sooner did the whale disappear than it shot up again. I caught my breath.

"Wow," whispered Sarah. "I don't believe in, you know, God or anything, but still."

"Totally," I said, knowing exactly what she meant. It's how I feel sometimes when I'm up in the mountains and it's really quiet and the light is falling in a certain way on the peaks across the canyon from you, and you feel—I don't even know what the right word is—whole, maybe. Like everything makes sense somehow.

After its third leap, the big whale headed away from us, and the little whales followed. I was afraid the boat would go after them—the thought of chasing and possibly scaring such amazing animals was awful—but we just continued in the same direction we'd been going.

Sarah turned around and leaned her back against the railing. "Okay," she said, "that was amazing."

"I know," said Jenna. "Each time I see it, I can't believe it."

Standing there with the two of them, the memory of the whales still alive on the back of my retinas, I felt happier than I could ever remember feeling. It was like my whole life had been leading up to that moment of the whale bursting out of the sea, drops of water shimmering off as it leaped to the sun. It made me want to be a great writer, to find the language to capture and communicate the feeling of perfect calm I was experiencing.

"Remember last summer when we came with Biff and Molly, and Molly puked the whole time and missed the whales?" said Sarah.

"Oh God," said Jenna. "I forgot about that. But I thought she ended up getting to see a whale at the end."

Sarah shook her head. "That was another trip. When she took the Dramamine."

"Poor Molly," said Jenna.

"Who's Molly?" I asked. I wondered if she was someone else they went to school with who summered up here. Maybe she'd become one of my new friends too.

"Adam's girlfriend," Sarah explained.

Still under the spell of the whales, I wasn't quite

following the conversation with my whole brain. "Adam who?" I said.

"Adam Carpenter," said Jenna. Then she punched me lightly on the arm. "Adam Adam. Our Adam."

"Oh," I said, suddenly interested. I still didn't know anything about Adam's dating history—here was clearly my chance to find out. "Adam went out with a girl named Molly?"

I swear, I hadn't meant my use of the past tense as a challenge, just a statement of fact. Adam used to go out with a girl named Molly. Now he was on a fishing trip thinking about me.

"Not *went*," corrected Jenna. "*Goes*. She spends the summer in New Hampshire with her family, but I think she's probably coming up in August like usual." She looked at Sarah to confirm.

"Far as I know," said Sarah.

It was like they were speaking a million miles away. I could barely hear them.

"Are you okay?" said Jenna. "Are you feeling sick?"

My knees were soft, and I wondered how much longer they would be able to support my weight. Adam had a girlfriend? *A girlfriend?* "I'm fine," I lied.

"That's what Molly said," said Sarah, slipping her hand under my elbow. "Then she went down below and we never saw her again."

169

"Let's get you to a seat," said Jenna, taking my other arm.

The three of us slowly made our way downstairs to a seat.

"I'll get you a ginger ale," said Jenna. "You look pretty green."

As she walked away, Sarah said, "You'll feel better as soon as we get on land."

"Sure," I said, wishing the thing that was making me sick were as temporary as our whale watch. "Sure."

There were no more whale sightings for the rest of the trip, so it didn't matter that Jenna and Sarah and I stayed below deck. I closed my eyes and leaned my head against the back of a bench, half hoping and half fearing I'd hear more about Molly.

They didn't mention her again, though. Not then, and not on the ride home. I know because even though I pretended to be asleep, I was listening the whole time.

IT RAINED NONSTOP for the next two days. I hoped wherever Adam and Lawrence were that it was raining there too, that their tent and their sleeping bags were soaked, that their boat had capsized. I hoped Adam got trench foot or whatever it is you get from wearing wet socks and shoes for too long.

I hoped he got gangrene.

I threw out *A Moveable Feast.* At dinner with her parents and my mom and Jamie the day after our whale watch, Sarah invited me to a movie with her and Jenna, but I was so afraid that if I went they would mention Molly *(Isn't she doing a modeling shoot at the end of the summer? Remember when she got that award for being the smartest, funniest person in the junior class? I can't recall—was it freshman or sophomore year that they were voted couple most likely to live happily ever?)* that I said I was still feeling sick from the boat trip.

It wasn't a lie either.

I felt like such an idiot. I ran our time together over

and over in my head until it felt as grainy as an old family movie. Why had I kissed him that night at the beach? Had he even wanted to kiss me back or had he just wanted to be polite? But if he'd just wanted to be polite, what about our day in Provincetown? What about *I like you too*?

He certainly hadn't acted like someone who was just being polite. I remembered his hands on my face in the car that night. *I can't stop kissing you.*

Why not, Adam? Because as long as your tongue's in someone's mouth, you can't talk about your *girlfriend*?

By Tuesday morning I was in the worst mood I'd been in for as long as I could remember. I knew Adam and Lawrence were coming back today or tomorrow, and just the idea of seeing Adam made my stomach knot up. What was I supposed to do when we all met up at Larkspur or The Clam Shack: feign interest in his fishing trip? Suddenly the fact that he hadn't told Lawrence he was with me in Provincetown made perfect sense. Of course he'd wanted to keep it secret—I was like his mistress or something.

I tried to think about how Lady Brett Ashley would have handled things if she'd found herself in my situation, but it was impossible. Lady Brett is never the *other* woman, she's always *the* woman. I mean, I'm not holding her up as some kind of moral compass, what with her having a lot of affairs and cheating on her fiancé all the time and everything. But the point is, she was never a victim.

How I'd managed to go from jaunty, potential girl-friend to victimized piece on the side, I'll never know. But here I was.

As if to mock my sour mood, the sun was shining brightly. When I went outside to go for a run, in the hope that endorphins pumping through my system might make me not feel like killing myself, my mom was sitting on the deck with her cell phone on her lap. I wondered if she was waiting for my dad to call, and for the first time since she'd dragged me across the country, I actually felt a little bit sorry for her. I mean, okay, it was annoying that she was so desperate for her hus-band's attention she'd go to these absurd lengths to get it, but wasn't it kind of lame that my dad wouldn't just give her the attention she wanted without her begging for it? Would it have killed my dad to, like, take his wife out for dinner once in a while or tell her she looked beautiful or just buy her a dozen roses if that's what she wanted? I mean, yes, it's dumb to want a watch or a pair of diamond earrings or a compliment about the sofa's new slipcovers as desperately as my mom appeared to want these things, but she *did* want these things and he *had* married her.

How did you end up as a forty-five-year-old woman 173

sitting by the phone waiting for it to ring like you were still in high school?

"Hi, honey," said my mom, turning around at the sound of the door sliding open.

"How'd you sleep?"

"Okay," I said. I gestured at the phone. "Are you waiting for Dad to call?"

"No, Jamie, actually," she said. "He went to town to buy fish for dinner tonight, and he's going to call and tell me what's available."

How creepy was it that my mom was waiting for a guy other than her husband to call? Was *anyone* faithful anymore?

"Jamie's so lame," I said.

"Why would you say that?" asked my mom. "He's a lovely man."

Now I was really getting irritated. It was one thing for Jamie to flirt with my mom, another for my mom to defend him to me.

Plus, I happen to hate the word *lovely*.

"What do you mean, he's *lovely*?" I said. "He's not *lovely*. He's trying to get with another man's wife. That's, like, the opposite of lovely."

"Katie, you're just being paranoid," she said. "We're old, old friends."

Paranoid? *Paranoid?* Paranoid like when I thought it was

significant that Adam didn't tell Lawrence I was sitting in

the restaurant with him? Was that the kind of paranoid my mother meant? "It's weird, Mom. You're married."

"I know I'm married, Katherine." My mom only calls me Katherine when she's completely annoyed with me. "Believe me, I'm spending a lot of time thinking about the fact that I'm married."

I don't know if I would have gotten so mad at her if I hadn't been so wildly pissed off at Adam even before the conversation started, but unfortunately I was, and I did.

"Oh really, mom? That's what you call spending all your time talking with Jamie and Henry and Tina about life in New York—'thinking about the fact that you're married'? If you're so bored and unhappy in Salt Lake, why don't you do something about your life instead of just pretending you're still some twenty-something single woman living with your friends in New York?"

"I'm not pretending anything, Kate."

"What are you going to do, leave Dad for Jamie? Be somebody else's wife? Why don't you take some responsibility for your choices instead of blaming it all on Dad and the fact that you're married to him?"

Her mouth dropped open. "You don't know anything about what you're saying," she said.

"All you want is some guy to make you feel important. Did it ever occur to you to maybe be a better role model for your daughters?" Even as the words came out of my mouth, I realized how absurd they were. I mean, 175 it wasn't my mom's fault that I'd been so happy when I'd thought Adam liked me. And it certainly wasn't her fault that he'd turned out to be with someone else.

"You watch your mouth, young lady!"

But I was on a roll. It felt so good to be yelling, I couldn't have stopped if I'd tried. "No, no I won't watch my mouth. 'Buy me this! Buy me that!' That's all you ever say. And then when Dad works hard to buy you the stupid stuff you want, you're like, 'Why are you working so hard? You should be admiring me more!'"

The last word had barely left my mouth when I felt my mother's hand smack against my cheek. The sound echoed in the air, sharp as a gunshot.

My mom and I looked at each other, then she folded her arms across her chest. "Don't speak to me until you're ready to apologize," she said.

I was crying, and it wasn't just because she'd hit me. I couldn't believe what I'd just said to my mom—it was really awful. But I couldn't take it back either. Just thinking about what a mean daughter I was made me cry even harder.

My mom stared at me. "I mean it," she said. Then she walked off the deck and up to the main house without another word.

I didn't see my mom for the rest of the day, which may have had something to do with my hiding out in the

Cooper-Melnick den watching old movies. At around four o'clock my phone rang, but it was Meg so I didn't pick up. I could already hear her lecturing me like some mini-mom. An hour later, when my phone rang again, I did pick it up. I knew my dad would at least listen to my version of the argument.

"Hey, Daddy," I said.

"Kate, I'm very disturbed by the things you said to your mother today," he said.

Of course. Nothing could unite my parents so effectively as the malfeasance of one of their daughters. Years ago, Meg took the car without permission (and without a license). The whole time my parents were outlining her punishment to her, they sat so close to each other and agreed with one another so passionately, you would have thought they were renewing their vows.

"Let me get this straight—you're mad that I told your wife not to flirt with another man?" This was really too much.

"Kate, that is not your place. You have no business implying your mother's behavior is inappropriate."

It wasn't like I didn't already feel bad about what I'd said to my mom. And who was my dad—the whole reason my mom was unhappy in the first place—to tell me I was the one who had upset her. "How about your behavior, Dad? How about how you never do anything she asks you to?"

"How about you don't talk to me that way, Katherine." My dad was really mad now, and I had the feeling that if we hadn't been separated by the better part of a continent, he might have slapped me too.

"Whatever, Dad," I said. "It's your messed up life."

As if he and my mom had compared notes, he echoed her threat to me. "Watch your mouth, young lady," he said. "You're treading on very thin ice."

"Yeah, well, I gotta go," I said. I was crying again, which was completely infuriating.

I hung up the phone and took *Casablanca* off pause. Ingrid Bergman's beautiful face filled the screen. "Play it, Sam," she said.

A shadow filled the doorway, and for a brief second I thought it might be my mom, but it was Sarah. "Hey, can I join you?" she asked, which was nice considering it was her house and everything.

"Sure."

Given that I hadn't talked to my best friend in over a week, the guy I'd thought was about to declare his love for me actually loved someone else, and both of my parents thought I was some kind of bad seed, there weren't many people in my life for me to watch a movie with.

I moved the empty DVD case to the arm of the couch to make room for her, but Sarah stayed where she was. It seemed kind of strange, but I figured it was none
178 of my business if she liked to watch TV standing in door-

ways. Just as I reached for the remote control, she suddenly blurted out, "I'm really sorry. About how I acted." Then she added, "When you first got here."

"Oh." I thought I should say something more, but I didn't know what, so I just said, "It's okay."

She made a face. "Not really," she said. "I'm kind of embarrassed. It's just . . ." she took a deep breath. "My mom was all gung ho about our being friends and it felt like there was all this pressure and . . .I don't know. It's not an excuse or anything. I should have just given you a chance, not made you prove how cool you are, you know?"

She was so gracious about apologizing, it made me want to be gracious back. I tried to picture what I would have done if my mom had announced that some random girl was coming to Salt Lake for the summer and I was expected to be her best friend while her mother had a nervous breakdown in my living room. "Don't feel bad," I said. "Seriously. If the situation had been reversed, I would have acted way worse."

"Well, that's nice of you to say," said Sarah. "But I'm still sorry."

"Thanks," I said. It was funny: I'd thought things with me and Sarah were okay, but now that she'd apologized, I realized her saying she was sorry was kind of a relief.

"So," she said, dropping onto the sofa next to me, "what are we watching?"

"*Casablanca*," I said.

"Oh, I love this movie."

When it ended, Sarah stretched her legs out in front of her and sighed contentedly. In spite of all the bad stuff that had happened over the past few days, Sarah's apologizing and our watching the movie together made me feel a little content, too. "It's the best," she said.

"I never get why Ingrid Bergman and Humphrey Bogart don't end up together," I said. "She doesn't love the other guy."

"You're a romantic," Sarah said.

I couldn't help the snort that escaped when she said that. Could you be a romantic when you'd been falling for someone else's boyfriend? I was pretty sure we had other names for that. . . .

"So, can I ask you something?" She sounded surprisingly hesitant for Sarah. I wondered if she was going to confide in me about Lawrence. On the one hand, I wanted us to be friends. On the other hand, I wasn't really up to hearing Sarah talk about how hard it was to have a guy you don't like that much be madly in love with you.

"Sure," I said.

"Well . . . I had this feeling about . . . something, and then my mom kind of confirmed it without realizing. I mean, she thought I knew."

Was this going to be about my mom and Jamie? I felt my stomach clench, remembering Jenna's comment the first day we'd met. *So, your parents are getting divorced?* What had Tina told Sarah?

"Yeah?" I said.

"The thing is, you seemed kind of shaken up when we talked about Molly, and then last night my mom mentioned that you and Adam went to Provincetown on Friday. And that you were . . . talking in Adam's car Thursday night when she and my dad came home."

My stomach didn't unclench now that it was clear she wasn't going to ask something about my parents. If anything, it just got tighter.

When I didn't respond, Sarah continued. "Is there something going on with you guys?"

Remembering how I'd once imagined this conversation going, I really felt for a second like I might puke. *He likes me. He's thinking about me on his fishing trip. I think we might be falling in love. . . .*

"Not anymore," I said. I'd been facing the blue screen of the television, but now I turned to face Sarah. I steeled myself to witness our mutual content evaporate. *Molly and I are like sisters. How could you mess with Adam; he and Molly are the most devoted couple since Romeo and Juliet. Get away from me you tacky slut.*

But she didn't say any of that. Instead she just let out a long low whistle. Then she said, "Are you okay?"

I totally did not want Sarah to see how upset I was about Adam, but a second later my chin was quivering, and a tear ran down my cheek and into my mouth. "I'm not crying about Adam," I said as about a million tears lined up to follow the first one. "I'm just having a really bad day."

"Sure," said Sarah. "I totally understand." She reached behind her for a box of tissues, then handed it to me.

"Thanks," I said, taking one out and blowing my nose.

"Do you feel like talking about it?"

I shook my head. The whole thing was so humiliating, what was there to say?

Sarah shrugged and patted me on the knee. "For what it's worth, those Carpenter boys are deadly," she said. "I have kind of a monster crush on Adam's brother, David."

"Really?" I was so surprised I stopped crying for a second. I totally could not imagine a guy Sarah liked not liking her back.

"Oh God," she said, half smiling, half wincing at something. "It's soooo bad. He's just this total outoorsy, hunky . . . man." She shivered as she said the word, and I knew that if Lawrence could have heard and seen her right now, he would have realized he didn't have a chance. "David Carpenter," she said. I remembered how I'd just wanted to say Adam's name the other day, and I knew that was what Sarah was doing now.

182   She continued, "He's got this girlfriend at Columbia.

She's older and just, like, perfect."

"But *you're* perfect," I said. As soon as the words were out of my mouth, I was embarrassed to have said them, but I also knew they were true. Sarah was so pretty and cool and chic and sexy. She was . . .

She was Lady Brett Ashley.

Sarah laughed. "Well, David doesn't seem to think so."

"He's crazy," I said.

"Totally," Sarah agreed.

"Do you think there's any ice cream?" I asked.

"My dad always has ice cream in the house," said Sarah. "It's like a holy law with him."

"I feel I need some ice cream," I said.

"If *you* don't need ice cream," said Sarah. "Who does?"

"Exactly."

We spent the rest of the afternoon eating ice cream and watching *To Catch a Thief*. And even though I was pretty sure my heart was broken, it ended up being not such a bad day.

Chapter 17

WHEN THE MOVIE ENDED, Sarah and I went out for pizza, and when we got back, all the grown-ups were out. I was sleeping when my mom came in, and she was already gone when I woke up. I felt bad about our fight. I knew I had to apologize, but I felt like I needed to do it in person, and we weren't exactly seeing a whole lot of each other. When my phone rang at nine, I thought maybe it was her calling, but it turned out to be Natasha's mom asking if I could do a lesson at ten. I headed up to the main house to look for my mother, but there was just a note from Tina to Sarah saying she and my mom and Henry had driven Jamie to Provincetown so he could catch the ferry to Boston and they'd be back by lunch.

Since the note didn't say that Tina and Henry would be back but my mother would be accompanying Jamie back to Boston and then to their new life together in New York, I couldn't not face the fact that my accusations had been just as outrageous as both of my parents had said they were.

Supposedly I was teaching tennis to Natasha, but in reality I was just giving myself whiplash. Every time I heard a guy's voice, I'd turn my head, looking for Adam. Finally, as I was looking toward the pro shop thinking I'd heard not Adam but my mom, Natasha returned a lob right onto my left cheek.

"Are you okay?" she asked.

"Yeah, sorry," I said, rubbing my cheek. "I'm just a little distracted." Like that wasn't totally obvious.

"Do you want to take a break?" she asked.

Since Mr. Davis was off somewhere, no doubt screaming into his cell phone at some hapless employee other than me, it wasn't like we *couldn't* take a break. Still, I felt a little bad about once again taking the man's money and not teaching his daughter tennis.

"Umm . . ."

"Five minutes," she said. She held up her hand, the fingers spread wide as if to show me what five was.

What the hell. It wasn't as if we were training for the U.S. Open or anything. "Sure," I said. "Five minutes."

"So," she said when we were sitting side by side on the bench, "what's on your mind?"

I couldn't help laughing. Here was Natasha trying to get to know *me*. "Just stupid stuff," I said.

"Like . . ." she prompted.

No way was I going to confess to a thirteen-year-old   185

girl what had happened with Adam. "Like I had a big fight with both my parents."

"Oh, yeah," said Natasha. "I know about that. My dad and I are basically in a perpetual fight."

No, really? "Because he's so into your being a tennis player?"

Natasha continued. "Because he's so into my being everything I'm not."

"Such as . . ."

She ticked every word off on a finger like each was an item on a shopping list. "Popular, adorable, a jock, a cute guy's girlfriend. You know, life as your basic, average, unrealistic teen movie."

"So what are you," I asked, "if you're not those things. Like, what are you into?"

"Nothing that involves the kids at my school," said Natasha. "The girls are total bitches and the boys are retarded."

"Yeah, well," I said, "I can't argue with the boys being retarded part." Natasha laughed. "But you still didn't answer my question." I pushed her gently in the shoulder. "What *do* you like?"

Natasha thought for a second. "I like writing poems. My mom doesn't mind, but it drives my dad crazy. He's all, 'What thirteen-year-old girl doesn't want friends and a boyfriend? Why do you spend all your time holed up in your room?'"

Considering where my latest foray into boyfriends had gotten me, I couldn't have disagreed more emphatically with her parents. Being holed up in your room was definitely where any sane thirteen-year-old girl should be.

"That's so cool that you write poems," I said. "I'm a writer too." Natasha looked at me, and for the first time there wasn't even the hint of a scowl to be found on her face. "Not poems, though," I added. "Short stories."

"That's cool too," said Natasha, and she nodded approvingly.

We sat there without talking, but the silence felt comfortable, not awkward. "So why don't you just tell your parents you don't want to play tennis?"

Natasha toyed with the strings of her racket. I could see her debating whether or not to tell me something, then she started talking. "It's just . . . you know how they used to do human sacrifices in ancient times?"

"Okay, I have *no* idea where you're going with this."

"Just hear me out." She looked up from her racket. "Tennis is like my sacrifice to my dad. If I take a couple of lessons a week, then he just bothers me about tennis. You know, 'Natasha, why aren't you practicing more? Natasha, why don't you take another lesson this week? Natasha, why aren't you entering the club championship?'" She snorted after she said *club championship*. "But if I don't take lessons, then he gets on my case about everything. 'Natasha, why aren't you outside enjoying this beautiful day? Natasha, wouldn't you like to have some of your friends over? Natasha, why don't you let your mother take you for a haircut and buy you a beautiful dress for the Labor Day dance.'" She was shaking her head at the thought of his haranguing her.

I remembered what my mom had said about my helping Natasha get closer to her dad, but given her description, what I really felt like doing was helping her get farther away from him. Still, I tried to think of something that might help them communicate. "Maybe you could show him your poetry or something?"

Natasha laughed. "My dad thinks poets are weird, that they all just grow up and stick their heads in the oven, like Sylvia Plath. No, it's better this way. Trust me."

"Well, what if you formed a writers' group with some people at your school. That way you'd both be happy. You'd get to write, but you'd be out of the house with other kids, like he wants you to be. That's what my writing teacher told me to do."

"And did you do it?" asked Natasha.

"Not exactly," I confessed.

"I rest my case."

I'd definitely run out of suggestions for her. "Do you want to play a little more?" I asked.

Natasha looked at the clock. "There's only ten

minutes left," she said. "Do you mind if we call it a day?"

Considering how far away from the court my mind was, I didn't feel like I should insist on our staying till the end of the hour. "Sure," I said.

"Let's have another lesson tomorrow," she said, reaching into her pocket and taking out a twenty dollar bill.

I laughed and pushed it back toward her. "Keep it," I said. "And we have to *play* tomorrow."

"Scout's honor—we'll play. I'm just really into this book I'm reading right now. But I'll be done by tomorrow."

"What are you reading?"

"*The Stranger*," she said. "It's about this French guy living in Algeria who thinks life is totally pointless."

"Well," I said, slipping my racket into the case. "I can't argue with that."

"See you tomorrow," said Natasha.

"See you tomorrow," I said.

I biked back to the house thinking maybe I'd find my mom there and be able to apologize, but she wasn't home. I wondered if Adam was back from his trip yet. I didn't want to wonder about him. I called Sarah at work.

"Do you want to have lunch or something?" I asked.

"That would be so fun," she said. "But I have to finish proofreading a pamphlet that's going to the 189 printers this afternoon. But do you want to go swimming later? Like at three? I should be done by then."

"Sure," I said, wondering what I'd do until three. "Maybe I'll go to the library." I was formulating the thought even as I spoke it.

"Perfect," she said. "I'll call you when I'm done and we'll go swimming."

As I pushed open the heavy glass library door, I forced myself not to think about the time I'd run into Adam here. Libraries were, like, my place. I felt at home in a library. Novels, writers, readers. These were my people. Who needed boys when you had books? I'd even brought my notebook and pen, thinking I'd do some work on my story.

I sat down at an empty table by the windows. There was a video lying there that someone had taken off the shelf and forgotten to put back. It was called *Gorillas in the Mist*, and it was about Dian Fossey, an American woman who apparently had lived in Rwanda studying gorillas for years. That didn't sound like such a bad life to me, being alone on a mountain with a bunch of apes. Let's face it—if a gorilla says *I can't stop kissing you*, your problems go way deeper than his possibly having a girlfriend you don't know about.

I opened my notebook and reread what I'd written so far, trying to imagine what direction Ms. Baker would tell me to take it in. But instead of Ms. Baker, I kept thinking about Adam. Where was he now? Was he thinking about me? I forced myself to focus on my story. *Details, Kate. Concrete details.* I gave the boy a baby sister he didn't like. I gave him a best friend who'd wanted to come on the trip but had gotten sick at the last minute. I'd just given him a nail-biting habit when I felt a hand on my shoulder. I looked up and there was Adam, and as soon as I saw him, I knew I'd only been writing with half my brain.

The other half had just been waiting for him.

Chapter 18

HE HAD ON THE SAME OXFORD SHIRT he'd been wearing the first time I ran into him in the library. I remembered how I'd wondered if I should take him seriously when he asked me out for a pop.

If only I hadn't taken him seriously about anything.

"Hi," he said.

"Hi," I said. I tried to pretend it was two weeks ago and nothing had ever happened between us and he was just some random guy friend of Sarah's, but it didn't work. My throat still felt dry and my heart was still racing.

"Can I talk to you for a minute?" he asked.

What could possibly be tackier than a tête-à-tête with somebody else's boyfriend? "I'm kind of busy right now," I said. I gestured at the notebook in front of me.

"Sarah told me," he said. "And she told me you were here." His voice was tight.

"I see," I said. I had no idea where those two words came from—I never say *I see*. But I liked how British it sounded.

"Can I just talk to you for a minute?" he asked.

Here's what I was not about to do: let Adam know this was a big deal. Which is why I said, "It's no big deal."

"Can I just talk to you for a minute?" he asked.

"It's no big deal," I said again. Would I ever be able to utter a sentence other than *It's no big deal*? "Really," I added, louder than I'd meant to.

Barbara the librarian looked over to where we were sitting and frowned. Then she put her finger to her lips.

Adam knelt down in front of me, and it struck me as ironic that he was in the position normally associated with a marriage proposal.

But of course marriage wasn't what Adam proposed. "Two minutes," he said, his voice a notch above a whisper. "Just give me two minutes." Then he added, "Please."

Of course I followed him outside to the little gazebo on the library lawn. Neither of us spoke as we walked. When we got to the gazebo, I sat down on one of the wrought-iron benches, and Adam stood leaning against the railing.

"What did Sarah and Jenna tell you?" asked Adam finally.

Since I already knew I wasn't going to emerge from this conversation with a boyfriend, it seemed to me the only thing I could hope to take from it was my dignity. "Just that, you know, you have a girlfriend," I said, impressed that I could utter the word without choking on it. "I hadn't known," I added, just to state the obvious. 193

"Right," said Adam. "So you're thinking I'm your basic asshole, right?"

I almost smiled at how accurate his assessment was. "Well," I said, "I'm not exactly fond of you right about now." *Fond of you?* It was like I was channeling Lady Brett Ashley without even trying. I folded my hands in my lap and crossed my ankles as if I were wearing a gray flannel pencil skirt and not jeans with a hole in one knee.

If Adam thought there was something weird about how I was talking, he didn't say so. "Look, just for the record, I'm not a total jerk, okay?" He ran his fingers through his hair, then rubbed his chin. "Molly and I are on a break this summer."

"On a break?" I repeated stupidly.

"Seeing other people," he explained. "We were having some problems, and she wanted to . . ." I finished the sentence in my head *and she wanted to break up with me, but I'm so madly in love with her that I convinced her we should take a break, not break up.* When I tuned back in, Adam was still talking. ". . . Look, you don't really want to hear this whole saga. But the point is, I wasn't, you know, cheating on her or anything."

The problem was this whole conversation was an out-of-body experience. I was watching myself talk to Adam, but I wasn't actually participating. "I see," I said.

"Do you?" he asked, coming over and sitting next to me. "Because I really like hanging out with you, and I got the feeling you liked hanging out with me too."

Hanging out. Was that what we were doing?

"Sure," was all I could come up with. He was so cute. Why was he so cute? His hair was damp, like maybe he'd showered right before coming over to find me.

To find me. He'd come to find me. He must like me. Yeah, for now.

"I mean, I guess I should have told you. I'm really sorry I didn't. But I didn't think you were the type to want a boyfriend or, you know, some big serious relationship." Was it my imagination, or did he say *big serious relationship* as if it were a repugnant political party I might be affiliated with. *I didn't think you were the type to be drawn to Nazism.*

What did he mean? What type of girl didn't want a boyfriend?

Let's see . . . um, probably a girl who'd announced that her role model was Lady Brett Ashley.

I mean, wasn't the whole point of being an independent jaunty woman that you didn't care about commitment or whether some random guy was your boyfriend? Hadn't I always planned to have dozens of meaningless affairs as I traveled the globe pursuing my writing career?

Well, here was Adam—ready, willing, and able to be the first in a long series of guys who meant nothing to me in the long run. I wasn't a victim, I was a good-time girl.

So what, exactly, was the problem?

"I think . . . I mean, I don't need to be serious," I said.

"Really?" he asked. He took my hand. "I mean, were you, you know, imagining this going beyond the summer?"

What did he honestly think I was going to say, given what I knew? *Yes, Adam, I fell in love with you the moment you quoted Hemingway to me. Ever since that night, I have dreamed of flying to New York the weekend of your senior prom, getting dressed with Jenna and Sarah and, draped head to toe in black* peu de soi, *descending the sweeping staircase of Sarah's exquisite town house to you, clad in a newly purchased tuxedo, standing on the bottom step and extending a single white rose in my direction.*

"God, no!" I said.

"Look," he said, "I don't want to influence your decision. The ball's in your court."

It was? How could the ball be in my court if he was the one with a girlfriend?

But he didn't have a girlfriend; he had a girl he was on a break with.

Still, clearly he wasn't in the market for a girlfriend.

But it wasn't like I was in the market for a boyfriend.

Was I?

What I *was*, right at this particular moment, was a little scared I might be losing my mind.

Adam reached over and slipped his arm under my legs, then swung my legs over his. He put his arms around my waist. "Okay, I'm influencing your decision," he said.

In spite of myself, I laughed. It felt so good to be sitting this close to him. I took a deep breath, smelling his shampoo and the clean sunshiny scent that must have been whatever laundry detergent his mom used.

I put my hands on his face and pulled him to me and we kissed. Kissing him was perfect. Who cared that he might be kissing some other girl come September?

Come September, I'd be halfway across the country.

We came up for air, noses bumping.

"You know what's funny?" I whispered.

"What?" he whispered back, kissing the corner of my mouth.

"Since you've been gone, I've managed to tell off both of my parents."

"Oh," he said, kissing me. Then he said, "Wait, why is that funny?"

I kissed him, tasting something sweet, like he'd recently eaten a lifesaver. Then I laughed. "I don't know," I said.

"Oh." He laughed too, then kissed me again.

It wasn't until we'd made a plan to meet up at Jenna's for a dinner the two of them were cooking and he'd dropped me off at home that I realized why it was funny that I'd told off both of my parents.

It was funny because the person I'd planned to tell off was Adam.

197

JENNA AND ADAM HAD BARBECUED an unbelievable meal—everyone's plate was piled high with tuna steaks, corn on the cob, and these amazing tomatoes and onions they'd grilled. We were sitting on Jenna's enormous back porch, which was surrounded by woods that might have been creepy if there hadn't been so many of us together and if there weren't the reassuring presence of Jenna's house behind us.

Adam had his arm draped casually over the back of my chair, and every once in a while he'd move his hand and touch my shoulder or run his fingers through my hair. I figured he must have told everyone about his and Molly's "break," because no one stood up and pointed a finger at him, shouting, *Get thee to hell, adulterer!* like some Old Testament prophet.

"This is delicious," I said to Jenna, gesturing with my fork at the grilled tomato I was eating.

"Thanks," she said. "But Adam made them."

"Oh, Adam, you're such a Renaissance man," said

198 Lawrence.

"So true," said Adam.

My mom's always talking about single men she meets in terms of whether or not they're a "catch." Not for *her* (despite the accusations I'd recently hurled in her direction); just in general. Like, last fall this doctor moved out to Salt Lake City, and he and my dad started playing tennis together, and my mom invited him to my parents' New Year's Eve party and then spent weeks—literally weeks!—trying to decide which of the single women she knew might appeal to him.

When I pointed out that women don't usually go in for arranged marriages, what with our living in the twenty-first-century United States, my mom just said, "Don't be ridiculous, Kate. He's a catch." She meant because he was single and a doctor and, I don't know, not a convicted sex offender.

Even though when she'd said it I'd just rolled my eyes and left her to her matchmaking, I found myself coming back to our conversation all through dinner at Jenna's. I thought of it when Jenna said Adam had grilled the vegetables and again when it was time to clear the table and Adam stood at the sink rinsing dishes before loading them into the dishwasher. And I thought of it right before we went home, when the lights went out and he went downstairs with a flashlight and found the panel with the circuit breakers and did whatever needed to be done to get the lights to go back on.

What I thought was, *Adam's a catch*.

And then I thought, *Too bad somebody's already caught him*.

On the way to my lesson with Natasha the next morning, I stopped by the pro shop to get a basket of balls. I wasn't exactly feeling chipper so much as I was feeling like a tree trunk that has been fed *through* a chipper, and when I saw Natasha sitting by the bench reading *The Fountainhead* and not wearing tennis whites, it didn't do much to improve my mood.

"Hey," I called out as I got near the bench.

It took her a long second to look up at me, and when she did, I could tell from the expression on her face that she was still deep in her book.

"Hi, Kate," she said.

I gestured at what she was wearing. "What gives? Where are your whites?"

Natasha gave me a conspiratorial smile. "Let's not play and say we did."

I was irritated, but I managed to keep my voice calm. "I'm not going to do that, Natasha. If you don't want to play tennis anymore, you need to tell your parents. I'm not going to take their money and not give you lessons."

I didn't realize Natasha hadn't been scowling until she scowled at me. "Lighten up, Kate. God."

I decided to ignore the implication that I was uptight.

"Do you have some whites you can change i┃
should we just cancel?"

"Oh yeah," said Natasha, "let me just reach ┃
pocket and grab out my white shorts." Her voice
dripped with sarcasm.

"Okay then," I said. "We'll do it another time."

I turned to walk away, but I only got a few feet before
Natasha yelled out, "What is your problem, Kate?"

"I don't have a problem, Natasha," I said, turning
around. "You're the one with the problem. You're the
one who's so pissed off at the world that you can't even
respect my time enough to put on a pair of stupid white
shorts and a white T-shirt."

"Ooooh, now I hurt your feelings? I didn't respect
you enough?"

I was so mad I could have punched something, but I
managed to keep my voice calm. "Natasha, I don't know
what your problem is. If you don't want to take tennis
with me, tell your parents to get you a new teacher. If
you don't want to play tennis at all, tell your parents and
deal with the consequences. Tell them you just want to
read and write poetry. But don't waste *my* time and your
dad's money."

Natasha stood up. "You know, not everyone is some
star tennis player with guys all over her, okay, Kate? Not
everyone can just do whatever she wants and say whatever she wants and still *get* whatever she wants." Her face

was bright red, and I could tell she was trying hard not to cry.

It took me a second to realize the star tennis player with guys all over her that Natasha was talking about was me. In spite of how mad I was, I couldn't help laughing. "Are you serious, Natasha? Do you really think that's who I am?"

"You know something, Kate, just forget it, okay? I thought you were cool, but you're so clearly not. So just . . . forget it." She was crying now and struggling to shove her book and bottle of water into her bag.

I felt really bad. "Natasha, wait." I took a step toward her, but when I put my hand on her shoulder, she shook me off.

"Look, just leave me alone, okay?" She got the book into the bag and jerked the strap onto her shoulder.

"Natasha, I want to talk to you," I said.

"Well, sucks for you," she said. And she stormed up the hill, leaving me standing there with a basket of balls and no one to hit them to.

I plopped down on the bench, totally defeated. The wood was hot, and the skin of my thighs burned for a minute when I sat down. How had things with Natasha gotten so out of control so fast?

Just then someone called my name, and I turned around. Adam and Lawrence were on the top of the steps that led down to the courts. They waved, then talked for a minute before Lawrence turned and headed into the pro shop. Adam jumped lightly down the steps and headed toward me. I remembered how happy I'd been to see him the last time we'd run into each other at the courts.

"I always think of tennis as a two-person game," he said, arriving at my side. "But I guess that's antiquated."

"I guess so," I said. After my fight with Natasha, I wasn't exactly in the mood to exchange witty banter.

"Where's your student?" he asked.

If only I were a really good liar and could say, *Oh, I'm not teaching a lesson. I'm meeting James.*

Who's James? Adam would ask, his voice tightening.

He's the other guy I'm dating. We love to play tennis together. You don't mind, do you, Adam? Adam, my God, calm down! Adam, why are you crying?

Despite how bummed out I was about fighting with Natasha, I made myself smile up at him. Let's face it—no one wants to "hang out" with an angry, cranky girl, right? "Where my student is is a very long and not very interesting story," I said. "Suffice it to say she's gone."

"Lucky me," he said. He twirled his racket. "Want to play a little? Lawrence just decided he's got to buy this new racket he tried yesterday."

"Sure," I said.

We made our way to opposite sides of the court, and

Adam served. It was a good serve—fast and low and just inside the box. Still, I slammed it back, feeling a surge of joy as it flew over the net. Adam returned the ball with a clean backhand that I just managed to return. It felt really good to be playing with someone who was my equal, when for the past two weeks the only person I'd played ("played") with was Natasha.

And then, as I raced back to the baseline and barely returned another fast low shot, I had a horrible thought.

Don't beat him. If you beat him, he won't like you.

I almost tripped, like the thought was a piece of detritus laying on the court. As the rally continued, it felt as if I had to literally push the idea out of my mind in order to return his shots. But it didn't go away, it just transformed itself. *He's a good player. Maybe you won't even have to pretend to lose. Maybe he's just better than you.*

And then suddenly he misjudged where a shot of mine was going to land. At the last second he realized his mistake, but even though he managed to scramble to the ball before it bounced a second time, his rushed stroke resulted in a lob so high and slow, hitting it was going to be a dream.

What was I supposed to do?

The seconds before I returned it seemed to play out in slow motion.

One.

Go for it.

I jogged backward to the baseline.

Two.

Let him win.

I sidestepped over to center court.

Three.

You're not the kind of girl who lets a guy beat her.

I centered myself behind where the ball was going to bounce.

Four.

You've never liked a guy enough to want to let him win.

I watched it land.

Five.

And I hope you never will.

I pulled my arm back and slammed my racket into the ball. It smacked down just over Adam's side of the net.

He ran to get it, but we both knew he didn't have a chance in hell of returning it.

"Nice shot!" he said, panting. He watched the ball bounce to the fence, then turned to me. I was amazed to see that his face, though red and sweaty, was plastered with a smile.

What did his smile mean? Was he impressed I'd beaten him?

Adam gestured toward where the ball had stopped. "Again?" he asked casually.

If he was happy with me when he lost, would he be

unhappy with me if he won? What, exactly, was riding on the next point? "Actually, I should go," I said. I was a little scared of how thoroughly confused playing tennis was suddenly making me.

"Are you sure?" he asked. "If you don't feel like playing, we could just hang out."

I couldn't hear the words *hang out* without thinking of our talk yesterday at the library. *I like hanging out with you, and I thought you liked hanging out with me too.* Less than twenty-four hours ago I'd been so sure I had this whole thing under control. What was happening to me?

I shook my head. "Sorry," I said. "I've gotta go."

"Sure," he said. He looked truly sorry I was going, which might have made me happy if I hadn't wanted *not* to be happy about his looking truly sorry I was going. "I'll see you later."

"Sure," I said. "Later." I gave what I hoped was a happy-go-lucky-good-time-girl wave and hauled ass out of there.

Chapter 20

SINCE I'D TOLD ADAM I had to go, I couldn't exactly hang out at Larkspur doing nothing for the rest of the day. I ended up just heading home. When I got there, our rental car was parked in the driveway. I made my way through the Cooper-Melnick house, finally finding my mom in the laundry room, where she was taking towels out of the dryer and folding them.

"Hi," I said. Her back was to me, and it was still a little weird to see her dark curly hair where for years I'd seen a blond bob.

"Hello," she said. Her voice was cool.

It was hard talking to her back, but I couldn't exactly blame her for not making this easy for me.

"Um, I just wanted to say I'm sorry. I shouldn't have said those things to you."

My mom turned around. She was actually smiling at me. "You did that very nicely," she said. "Apology accepted."

I was truly grateful to her for being so nice about it.

Some of the things I'd said to her had been awful enough that I winced just thinking about them. "Thanks," I said. Then I added, "I wasn't really mad at you."

"Who were you mad at?"

The last person I'd meant to confide the Adam story in was my mother, but before I could stop myself, the whole thing came pouring out of me.

"Oh, sweetheart," she said. Then she stepped toward me and we hugged. It was actually kind of nice. My mom wears this perfume that doesn't smell flowery at all, just crisp and citrusy. It makes me think of hiking through the woods on a cool, fall day. And she really hugs you when she hugs you. Normally I pull away before she's done hugging, but this time I didn't.

I lifted myself up so I was sitting on the washing machine. I didn't want to think about Adam and Molly anymore. "Let's talk about something else," I said.

My mom looked at me for a long time, but she didn't tuck my hair behind my ears or say anything about it being too long, like she normally does. Then she put her hands on my knees and took a deep breath. "I do have something I need to talk to you about, actually."

Her voice was serious; suddenly I wasn't so sure I wanted to hear whatever it was she wanted to say.

"It's . . . about me and your dad. We're . . ." Her
eyes welled up, and she shook her head hard, as if

that would make them stop. To my surprise it worked—she didn't start crying. "We're not in a great place."

"What do you mean?" I said. Out of nowhere, I felt my own eyes start to sting.

"Kate, I know you think I came out here on a whim. That I was just . . . throwing a hissy fit or something." She smiled when she said it, but I cringed a little at her landing on the exact words I'd used to describe her behavior to myself. "The truth is, I've been very, very unhappy for a long time. I think we both have—your father and I. Only he just works hard and hopes things will get better, and I can't do that. Even if I had a job, I couldn't do that," she added quickly.

"I wasn't going to say anything about your having a job," I said, which was true.

"The point is, you're right—I do need more in my life than just you and Meg and your dad. But even if I have those things . . ." Her voice started to shake, and she took a deep breath. "Even if I have those things, I'm not sure that we're going to be able to work things out."

I was crying for real now. "You mean you might get divorced?!" How could my parents get divorced? I mean, I knew they weren't exactly the perfect couple or anything. But divorce?

"I don't know, sweetheart," said my mom, and she was crying too. "It's not what either of us wants. But neither of us wants to be unhappy either." She put her 209 arms around me. Since I was sitting on the washer, I was a little taller than she was, and I put my head on her shoulder and just bawled. I kept thinking about how mad my dad had been when we were on the phone the last time. Was that what our family was going to be like from now on—people who just yelled mean things and accusations at each other?

Were we technically even going to *be* a family anymore?

The thought made me cry harder, and for a minute it was like I almost forgot my mom was even there. But then I realized she was patting me on the back and humming a little. It was the kind of thing you might do to a little kid, or even a baby, but it actually made me feel better.

Finally I pulled away from her. "I'm sorry," I said. "I got you all snotty and wet."

She laughed and brushed at her eyes with the back of her hands. "I used to change your diapers," she said. "A little snot's not a big deal."

"So what happens now?" I asked.

She handed me a washcloth still warm from the dryer, and I wiped my face with it. "I honestly don't know," she said. "We're trying to figure out what the next step is. So I'm going to have to ask you to be patient and understanding for a little while longer. Do you think you can do that?"

I nodded. "Of course," I said.

What I didn't say was that things had been a whole lot simpler when I'd been convinced my mom was just being a prima donna.

I headed to the guesthouse and got into bed with *Lolita*, even though it was still the middle of the day. Sarah knocked at the door around six and said she and Jenna were going to play mini golf, but I pretended I was napping. My mom invited me to go to the movies and dinner with her and Henry and Tina, but I told her I wanted to be by myself.

I tried to read, but I couldn't focus on the words in front of me. Divorced. My parents might get divorced. Who would I live with, my mom or my dad? Before this trip, the answer would have been a no-brainer (*Hello, Dad!*), but now I wasn't so sure. I thought of how he hadn't called me back after our fight, how he'd been too busy to talk almost every time I'd called him from Cape Cod. Maybe my mom and sister were right. Maybe he was a little selfish.

What if they did some kind of joint-custody thing and I had to change houses every few days? Where would I keep my stuff?

Just as I was wondering if my mom would stay in our house and my dad would get an apartment, or if it would go the other way around, Jamie's invitation to my mom 211 rang in my ears, and I realized just how big my parents' geographic split could potentially be. *Do you ever think about coming back East?* What if my mom decided not to move across town but across the country?

I couldn't believe I was lying there trying to figure out what *state* I'd be living come September—this wasn't possible. It wasn't happening.

I needed to talk to someone. I dug my cell out of my bag to call Laura, but then stopped before I could dial her number. It wasn't just Brad that made me not want to talk to my best friend. So much had happened since the last time we'd had a conversation—I'd have to tell her about everything: the fight my mom and I had, which meant explaining about why I'd been in such a bad mood, which meant explaining about Adam. Just thinking about getting her up to speed felt exhausting.

And then, almost without consciously deciding to call her, I dialed Meg's number.

"Hey," she said, picking up on the first ring. "Long time no talk."

"Hey," I said. "Did you know that Mom and Dad might get divorced?"

Meg took a long deep breath. "I knew Mom was really unhappy," she said. "I knew she'd come East to try and decide what to do."

"I knew that too," I said. "But I didn't *know* it. I mean, I didn't take it seriously. I didn't believe it."

I thought Meg was going to say something about how I should have listened to Mom more carefully, but instead she laughed. "You know something, I don't think I believed it either."

"Really?" I was totally surprised.

"Really," she said. "I still don't believe it. I still hope they're going to work things out."

"Well, Mom said they might. She said they both want to."

"Yeah, I wouldn't get your hopes up, Katie." I felt a tiny bit irritated by her saying that. I mean, she didn't *know*. Then again, maybe if I'd listened to her assessments of my parents' marriage earlier, I wouldn't have been the victim of a drive-by reality check in the laundry room earlier.

"I'm kind of mad at Dad," I said. "We had a fight a couple of days ago, and at the end I was crying, and he didn't even call me back or anything."

I immediately regretted telling Meg. I knew she was going to say something mean about Dad.

But to my surprise she just said, "I'm really sorry, Katie. That sucks."

"Yeah," I said. "It does, doesn't it?"

We talked a little more, not even about Mom and Dad, just about what I was reading and the class she was taking, and then we said good-bye.

And for the first time in as long as I could remember, after we hung up, I was glad I'd called her.

* * *

I read for a while, and I'd just decided to go to sleep (it was only around nine o'clock, but it wasn't like I had anything to stay up for) when there was a knock on the door. It was spooky, actually. My mom and Tina and Henry hadn't gotten home yet, and I didn't think Sarah had either. What if there was some kind of serial killer on the loose? I made myself a little smaller on the bed, trying to remember if the door was locked or not. There was another knock, and I realized I didn't even know the address of the house I was staying in. How could I call 911 and just tell them I was in the Cooper-Melnick house somewhere by the bay?

I was so dead.

"Kate? It's me."

It was Adam. My heart started pounding even harder than it had when I'd thought I was about to be the victim of an ax murderer.

"Just a sec," I said. Of course I looked like total crap. My hair was up in a tight ponytail, and I wasn't exactly supermodel chic in my sweats. If life were a romantic comedy I would have had a face mask on for good measure; but as I now knew, it was not. A romantic *farce*, maybe, but not a comedy.

I opened the door. Adam looked impossibly cute in a dark blue fleece and a pair of ancient Levis with a patch on the knee.

"Hey," he said. He was smiling our secret smile.

"Hey," I said as casually as I could.

"How come you guys didn't come by the Shack?" he asked, clearly assuming I'd been playing mini golf with Jenna and Sarah.

It was too complicated to explain that I didn't know why Jenna and Sarah hadn't come by since I hadn't been with them, so I just said, "You know, I just wasn't hungry." *Because that's the kind of cool, casual, love-it-or-leave-it kind of girl I am. Sometimes I'm hungry for lobster, sometimes I'm not.*

"I wanted you to meet my brother. He came in this afternoon." Adam looked really happy about his brother's arrival. All I could think of was how there had been a time I'd been shocked to have kissed a guy who had a brother I didn't know about.

If only a brother had been the one thing I hadn't known Adam had.

We were still standing in the tiny vestibule. I was simultaneously so happy and so sad to see him—it was like he was something precious and beautiful and delicate of mine that I'd recently discovered had a huge crack running down the middle of it.

"Come with me," he said, blissfully unaware of my thoughts.

What was I supposed to say? I mean, it wasn't like I could claim a prior obligation. "I'm—" I gestured vaguely at what I was wearing, wishing I were in something more officially pajamay so I could plead inappropriate attire.

"Come on," he said, pulling at my hand. "I want to show you something."

"Okay," I said. I slipped on a pair of flip-flops that were right in the entrance area, not realizing until I'd pulled the door shut behind me that they were my mom's and, therefore, about a size too small. I could feel my heels hitting the gravel as we walked down the drive-way and headed for the woods.

No doubt there was symbolic meaning to be found in this, but if so, I wasn't in the mood to find it.

It was incredibly quiet and dark in the woods, though every once in a while bright moonlight would break through the trees and a patch of ground would be illu-minated as clearly as if it were spotlit. Neither Adam nor I spoke, leaving the vaguely creepy silence intact. I thought of this line from a poem we'd had to memorize freshman year. "The woods are lovely, dark and deep." It was a perfect description, and I thought I remembered our teacher saying the author was from New England somewhere. I wondered if he'd been talking about woods in Massachusetts, woods like the ones I was in right now.

Adam led me down the lane that went from the

driveway out to Route 6. But instead of going left, the

way I'd always gone, we went right. A couple of hundred yards after we turned, he turned again, this time onto a tiny narrow path.

"Stay close," he said. "There's poison ivy."

I could barely make out his shadow even though he was only about two feet in front of me; but within just a few steps, it started getting lighter. Less than a minute after his warning about the poison ivy, we were standing in a little clearing. I took my eyes off Adam's back and realized we were by the side of a large pond.

"Oh wow," I said. The full moon was reflected in the surface of the perfectly still water. Looking up I saw the sky, impossibly busy with stars made pale by the brightness of the moon's light.

"I know," said Adam. "It's amazing, right? This is my favorite spot on Cape Cod."

I could see why. After the impossible immensity of the Atlantic Ocean and the dreamy beauty of the bay, the pond was intimate and safe. It reminded me a little of places I'd come upon hiking in the mountains around Salt Lake City. Though we were at sea level, this could have been a mountain pond. Suddenly I felt a wave of homesickness. When I realized that the home I was missing might never be what it had been, I felt dizzy with sadness.

Adam pulled me in front of him and put his arms around my waist. He nestled his chin on my head. "My house is right over there," he said, pointing across the lake. "If it were day you could see it."

"Really?" I said.

"Well, if it were day and there weren't any trees." He thought for a second. "And you had a telescope." He laughed. "And X-ray vision."

This is so romantic, I thought. This is the most romantic thing that's ever happened to me.

"If it weren't freezing, I'd say we should go skinny-dipping," he said. "As it is, I'm way too much of a wimp."

He turned me around gently, and we started kissing. It felt so great to be kissing Adam. Who cared about my parents' marriage? Who cared that I was never going to be Adam's girlfriend?

But then he slid his hands up my back and hugged me close to him, and instead of feeling great, I felt like I was going to start bawling.

Apparently this good-time girl wasn't having such a good time.

"I'm sorry," I said, pulling away. "I can't do this."

Adam had his hands in my hair, so our heads were still really close together. "Can't do what?" he whispered.

I didn't say anything for a second, just put my hands on his wrists and pulled them out of my hair. "This," I said. "I want us to stop . . . hanging out."

"Oh," he said. Then he said it again. "Oh." He took a step back from me. "Did I do something?"

"No," I said quickly. "I just . . . think . . . I mean, I *don't* think . . ."

He didn't wait for me to finish my sentence. "Why?" he asked.

What was I supposed to say? *Because I'm not as cool as you think I am. Because I really, really like you and I can't spend one more second pretending not to care that even if you like me too, you also like somebody else. Because I just had some really bad news about my family and I don't want to kiss somebody if I can't tell him about it.*

Did the sad fact that I couldn't manage to act like Lady Brett Ashley mean I had to be her polar opposite: Lady Kate Loser?

"No reason," I said. I hoped my voice didn't betray the fact that I was about ten seconds away from crying.

He didn't say anything for a minute, and I took a couple of quiet deep breaths. If this went on much longer, I was definitely going to lose it. Finally he looked up at the sky and gave a little laugh. "Not having fun anymore, hunh?"

"Right," I said, nearly choking on the word.

"Well, I can't argue with that," he said.

Please, argue with it.

I didn't say anything.

"I'll take you home," he said. I followed him back the way we'd come. The walk to the house felt much shorter than the walk to the pond had. Neither of us spoke this time either, though it was a very different silence from our earlier one.

The trees thinned and then we were walking up Tina and Henry's driveway. An outdoor light was on next to the main house, and the lamp I'd been reading with cast a glow through the glass doors of the guesthouse.

"Here you are, safe and sound," he said. Despite the lights and the moon, it was too dark to see his face clearly.

"Thanks," I said. "I—" What was I going to say, *I had fun tonight?*

Um, not.

But he was already walking purposefully toward his car, about as upset about our "breakup" as he would have been by a badly cooked lobster. "Good night," he said.

"Good night," I said. I'd been going for breezy, but my throat was a little too tight for that.

Chapter 21

I WOKE UP THE NEXT MORNING to the sound of the shower running. I felt about as low as I had all summer. I thought about my parents. I thought about Adam. I missed him already. Less than twelve hours had passed since I'd told him things with us were over, and I wasn't sure how I was going to make it through the day without seeing him. Not to mention how, if and when I did see him, I wasn't going to *see* him. We'd just say *Hello* or *What's up* and go our separate ways. Maybe I hadn't been his girlfriend before last night, but at least I'd been his . . . something. Being Adam's nothing felt way worse than being his something had.

My mom came out of the bathroom in her robe, her hair wrapped in a towel.

"Morning," she said. "Did you sleep well?"

"I guess," I said. "Did you have a good night?"

She shrugged. "I guess," she said. Then she looked at me a little more closely. "Are you okay?"

I shook my head, not trusting myself to talk. My 221

mom came over and sat on the edge of the bed. "Is this about me and your dad?" she asked.

"Kind of," I said. "And Adam." I told her about breaking up with him last night. If you could even call it a breakup, what with our never having been officially going out.

"Oh, sweetheart," she said. She just sat there for a minute stroking my hair. Then she said, "You know what I think? I think you really like this boy. And I think you shouldn't worry so much about what's going on with that other girl. He obviously likes you a lot. Why don't you tell him how you feel? Maybe he'll surprise you."

"I highly doubt it," I said. It's all fine and good to talk about, like, expressing your feelings when you're married to someone and you're in your forties. It's a little different when you're a teenager and you're not even a couple with the other person.

"What do you have to lose?"

Oh, I don't know. My dignity. The perfect illusion I have managed to create that I'm this incredibly cool, awesome girl.

Instead of explaining to my mom all the reasons I could never tell Adam how I really felt, I just said, "I think I'm going to go for a run."

"Okay," she said. But when I was leaving the house, she added, "Don't try to be somebody you're not, Katie. Give Adam a chance to know the real you."

"Maybe," I said, even though I knew there wasn't a

snowball's chance in hell of my doing that. If Adam liked me at all it was because I was cool and fun. He wasn't going to like me more if I revealed to him that I was needy and sad.

I ran down the driveway and made a right. *Faster. Faster.* As I passed the turnoff for the pond, I could practically feel Adam's lips on mine, his hands on my face. I shook my head hard to clear my mind of the image, but each time I got rid of it, another one would take its place. Adam smiling at me on the tennis court. Adam's foot entwined with mine under the table at The Clam Shack. Adam. Adam. Adam.

I missed him so much—it was like he was a drug I was addicted to or something. The more I thought about never kissing him again, the sadder I got. The trees shimmered in the bright sun, reminding me of the moonlight from last night. I looked up and nearly fell into a big pothole in the sandy road. I dropped my eyes from the sky. I needed to watch where I was going.

A few yards in front of me the road divided, and I realized I had no idea where I was. Perfect. I wanted to be lost. Maybe I'd get so turned around that I'd never find my way home, just wander aimlessly in the woods of Cape Cod for the rest of my life. Of course, the proliferation of houses in the vicinity made that fairly unlikely. Nailed to the enormous tree next to me were half a dozen little plaques with names and arrows pointing up the narrow road to my right, and I was sure someone at the *Jones*, *Miller*, or *Zuprinsky* households would be happy to offer me sanctuary and a free phone call. If not, I could always turn to the *Graham* family. Or I could ask the *Carpenters*.

Carpenter.

My heart pounded in my chest, only it wasn't from the run. This could not be a coincidence. My mom had just told me to tell Adam my true feelings, to give him a chance, and here I was literally at a fork in the road with an actual sign right in front of me. A sign directing me to Adam's house. A house I could probably never in a million years have found if I'd set out in search of it.

I stood there, paralyzed.

The same poet who wrote the thing about the woods being lovely, dark and deep also had a poem that went, "Two roads diverged in a yellow wood" (I guess he spent a lot of time in the woods). In the end, he said, he was glad to have taken the road less traveled. Okay, clearly only a small percentage of the people who traveled this road were headed to Adam's family's house, but even in my confused state I knew you couldn't interpret a poem that literally.

I started to jog slowly in place. Thinking about poetry made me think about Natasha and how she thought I was this confident ace tennis player with guys all over me. Wouldn't a girl like that just go for it? Just tell Adam the truth? *I like you, Adam. I really, really like you. I don't just want to be the girl you hooked up with. I want to be the girl you go out with.*

No. This was insane. I'd made my decision. I couldn't spend the summer trying to make Adam fall in love with me, wondering every second what he was thinking: if he was finding me as funny or charming or pretty as his real girlfriend. Given the circumstances, how could I possibly tell him how I felt?

And given that, the only way to be with him was to pretend I didn't mind fooling around with a guy I really liked who didn't really like me back. The only logical solution had been to end it, and so I'd ended it.

I turned to the right and started running.

And then, before I'd gone a hundred yards, I turned back.

The problem is, liking someone is a lot of things.

But logical isn't one of them.

The road to Adam's house wound up and around a slight hill—one of the only ones I'd climbed since arriving on Cape Cod. I passed a couple of driveways or possibly small roads but didn't see the name Carpenter again. Now that I'd decided to go to Adam's, the thought of not being able to get there made me crazy. I was afraid if I didn't find his house soon, I might have to stand there in the middle of the woods screaming, *Adam!*

Adam! like Stanley Kowalski in *A Streetcar Named Desire*.

Had I passed it? What with my being more or less out of my mind with agitation and anxiety, it wouldn't have been hard to miss something, even something as big as a house. Just as I was wondering if I should retrace my steps to the bottom of the hill and head up it again, the trees thinned, and I realized that at some point what had been a road had become a driveway, and I was now, almost definitely, running on Adam's property.

The driveway came to an abrupt end practically at the front door of a beautiful modern cylindrical house, taller than it was wide. There were decks poking off at unexpected intervals, and across a clearing there was what must have been a guesthouse, since it was a smaller version of the same structure.

In my decision to find Adam, I'd only taken things as far as my arrival. Now that I was here, I wasn't sure what to do. Should I ring the bell? What if his mom answered? For some reason I pictured Mrs. Carpenter loving Molly, which made it hard to see myself casually asking her if Adam was home. *I know what you're planning! Stay away from my son, you shameless hussy!*

I must have been standing in front of the house for a full five minutes when I realized I could hear someone talking on the phone. I cupped my hand behind my ear and listened. It sounded like the person was outside, and I followed the voice around to the side of the house. There were steps up to a deck, and I climbed them, hoping Adam's family wasn't the type to prosecute trespassers.

I peered around the side of the house, and there he was sitting in an Adirondack chair with his back to me and his feet up on the rail of the deck. My heart began to pound even harder than it had been, which I would have said was impossible. On his feet was a pair of sneakers I hadn't seen him in before, but I recognized his sweater as the one he'd lent me at the Fourth of July bonfire.

"No, seriously?" he said into the phone. Then he laughed. I loved his laugh. I'd fight some stupid girl named Molly to the death for that laugh.

As I stood there listening to and loving Adam's laugh, I realized I was also eavesdropping. But I wasn't sure what to do about it. Should I call his name so he'd turn and see me? Then again, it might be kind of freaky to turn around and find someone standing on your deck. Or maybe that was only freaky if you were a girl, since you had to worry that the person who'd climbed onto the deck to be with you was none other than the friendly neighborhood peeping Tom.

I decided to go back around to the front of the house and ring the bell; better safe than sorry. I took a step back in the direction I'd come.

"All right, man, we'll talk later."

There was a creak that could only mean he was standing up. I took another step. Should I run? But how weird was that? *Wait, is that you racing off my back deck, Kate?* While I realize sometimes the best defense is a good offense, it doesn't necessarily follow that the best entrance is an exit.

"Yeah, yeah, definitely," he said. "Okay, bye."

One more step and I'd be out of his line of vision. I put my right foot onto the top stair and—

"Hello?"

I was so keyed up, I was pretty sure my body was giving off an audible hum. I took a deep breath and tried to turn around, but it was like I was frozen to the spot. No way was I going to be able to say this to his face.

But I couldn't just stand there not looking at him *and* not talking.

"Listen," I said finally, "I'm not going to turn around because I just want to say this really fast without looking at you, okay?"

"Are you—"

I could practically hear the smile in his voice, which was enough to completely derail me. I just liked him so much. "Don't interrupt me, okay? I only want to say one thing and then I'll go if you want me to." I took a deep breath and focused on a small piece of wood sticking out of the banister. I dug under it with my thumb. "The thing is, I really like you. I liked you the entire time, only I was trying to be . . . I don't know, cool about the whole Molly thing."

"Wait a minute," he said.

"No!" I said. "Look, if I don't say this now, I'm never going to say it. And I really want to say it because the answer to your question—I mean, it's a pretty old question, so you probably don't even remember asking it, but the answer is that yes, I did think this could be some big serious thing , even if it couldn't go beyond the summer, and . . . well . . ." Now that I'd started, telling Adam how I felt wasn't scary, it was wonderful. Nothing that felt this wonderful could be bad. "So that's why I broke up with you last night. I know it sounds completely perverse, but I broke up with you because I like you so much. I wanted to be the kind of girl who's too cool to admit that, but I guess I'm not. I don't know what kind of girl I am, but I'm not her." It was as if a ten-thousand-pound weight had just fallen from my shoulders; I'd never felt so light. "Okay. You can talk now."

There was a pause, and then he said, "Are you . . . I think you're looking for Adam?"

I spun around.

The person standing in front of me was most definitely not Adam. He was wearing Adam's sweater. And he had hair like Adam's. And he was more or less as tall as Adam was. But that's where the resemblance ended. The guy standing in front of me had a full beard and glasses. I mean, maybe if he shaved the beard and got a pair of contacts he would look more like Adam, but he still wouldn't *be* Adam.

"Oh my God," I said.

"I'm David," he said. "I'm Adam's brother."

"Oh my God," I said again.

"I'm really sorry," he said. "I tried to——"

"Oh my God," I said for the third time.

"Adam left for New Hampshire early this morning," he said. Then, as if it made a difference to me, as if the humiliation factor of my current situation hinged on Adam's departure time, he added, "He got up at six."

New Hampshire? New Hampshire?! New Hampshire was where Sarah and Jenna had said Molly was for the summer. In other words, last night, while I'd been lying on my bed, brokenhearted, Adam had been plotting his reunion with his girlfriend. While I'd been confessing my love for Adam to his brother, he'd been confessing his love for Molly to Molly.

"I have to go," I said.

"I'm really sorry," said David. He didn't have Adam's face, but he had a nice face, and I could tell he honestly felt bad about the part he'd played in my romantic self-immolation. Which somehow only made what I'd just done feel even worse.

I shot off the deck and down the driveway as fast as if I were being chased. Maybe if I'd been less embarrassed I could have cried or screamed, but as it was, all I could do was say *Oh my God Oh my God Oh my God* over and over in my head, like a chant. It drowned out the music blasting on my iPod, my feet pounding against the sandy road, even my heart hammering against my ribs. I came to the bottom of the hill and shot past the sign for Adam's house. Had I actually thought it was a *sign* and not a sign?

I pictured David calling Adam, the two of them talking about what I'd said and pitying me for having said it. Then I thought about how fast Molly would want to reconcile with Adam now that there was another girl after him. It was like I'd done the one thing guaranteed to get Adam back together with his girlfriend.

Talk about signs. I needed one for my forehead:

Total idiot.

Chapter 22

EVEN IF I HADN'T JUST ENDURED the most humiliating experience of my life, I still wouldn't have been prepared for what I walked in on when I got home. Because what I saw when I opened the door to the guesthouse was my mother packing her suitcase.

"Are we going somewhere?" If only. If only my mom had decided she wanted us to keep moving around the country, like Lolita and Humbert Humbert.

My mom gestured for me to sit on the couch. Even though I was pretty sweaty and gross, she sat down next to me and put her arm around me. "I just booked myself a flight to Salt Lake out of Logan for early tomorrow morning, so I'm going to spend the night in Boston. I talked to your dad, and I think he and I need to have some face time if we're going to figure out what comes next."

"Oh," I said. It was like I'd been gone for forty-five days, not forty-five minutes. "So this is it."

"This is something," said my mom. "I'm not sure

what, exactly. But yes, your dad and I have some decisions to make."

"Wow," I said. "Am I . . . should I be packing too?"

My mom leaned against the back of the couch. "I reserved you a seat," she said. "But I didn't book it. The truth is, I'd like a little time alone with your dad. But I also don't think it's fair to make you stay here if I'm going back. So the decision is yours. I'd like to leave for Boston after lunch."

"Wow," I said again. How tempting was it to just start packing, to say good-bye to the disaster that was Adam and Natasha and basically every single aspect of my summer east of the Mississippi?

But my mom and dad needed time alone together. She'd just said that. Was I really going to risk my parents' marriage so I didn't have to deal with the spectacular wreckage I'd managed to make of almost all the relationships I'd formed here?

"No," I said slowly. "You go."

"Are you sure?" she asked. "I know you're having a little bit of a tough time here right now. I don't want you to have to stay if it's going to make you unhappy."

You don't know the half of it, I thought.

"I'm sure," I said. "You should go and I should stay." I was afraid if I told my mom what had just happened with David she'd feel bad and tell me to come home with her.

And I knew I wouldn't have the courage to say no again.

My mom went back to packing, and I went out to the deck. Standing there looking at the bay, I tried to convince myself that I'd be okay on Cape Cod without her. It was beautiful. Sarah and Jenna were my friends. Okay, I could never face Adam or his brother again, but how hard could it be to avoid them just because the only people I knew within a thousand miles were people we had in common.

Luckily my phone rang before I could get too hysterical about what the rest of my summer was going to be like. It was a Cape Cod number; I recognized the area code.

"Hello?" I said.

"Kate?" said a female voice.

"Yes."

"It's Natasha."

My heart started hammering. "Natasha," I said. "Hi."

She spoke quickly. "I got your number from my mom. I'm really sorry."

"What?" I said, confused. "You don't need to be sorry about calling."

"No," she said. "I mean I'm sorry about what I said."

"No, I'm sorry," I said. I sat down and covered my face with my hand, even though she couldn't see me. "I handled everything so badly. I was just really angry

about . . . something else."

She laughed. "Yeah, I think I was too."

There was a pause, and then I said, "So do you want to have another lesson?"

"I don't think so," she said. And even though I didn't exactly blame her, I couldn't help feeling disappointed.

"Sure," I said. "I understand."

"But I *do* want to form a writers' group," she said.

"What?" I said, even though I'd heard her.

"I said, 'I do want to form a writers' group.' So are you in or out?"

"Um . . ." Natasha was younger than I was, but she seemed pretty smart. And she was definitely serious about reading and writing.

"Come on," said Natasha. "What do you have to lose?"

It was true. What did I have to lose?

"Okay," I said, and just saying it made me feel happy. Maybe I could never face Adam again, but at least I hadn't totally destroyed my relationship with Natasha.

I pushed Adam out of my mind. "Okay," I said again. "Let's meet the day after tomorrow. That will give us time to write something." The thought of having a deadline got me excited.

"First assignment?" asked Natasha.

"Hang on a second," I said. I went inside and dug the book Ms. Baker had given me out of the bottom of my underwear drawer, where it had lain, untouched, ever since I'd unpacked it. I flipped through the pages, each of which had a number and a writing exercise on it. A few were cool, like the one that said "Write a story entirely in dialogue," but they didn't seem as if they would work for both poetry and prose. When I hit page twenty-five, I almost laughed out loud. Then I went outside and picked up the phone.

"Ready?" I said.

"Ready," said Natasha.

"'Write about a trip from the perspective of somebody who doesn't want to take it,'" I read.

"Oh, that's good," said Natasha. She thought for a second. "I'm going to write a poem about how when it's cold I hate getting out of bed to pee in the middle of the night."

I laughed. "Excellent." I was impressed by how fast she'd come up with the idea.

"So I'll see you Sunday," she said. "What time?"

In case I wanted to have the morning to write, I said, "Four o'clock."

"Library?" she asked.

"Actually," I said, "let's meet at the gazebo outside the library. I need to reclaim it."

"From what?" she asked.

"It's a long story," I said.

"Cool," said Natasha. "Maybe you'll write it someday."

"You know, maybe I will."

Chapter 23

MY MOM AND TINA AND I went for lunch at this little burger place on Route 6, and then my mom hugged us both and turned the car west, toward Boston, while we headed east, to the house. It was really weird to drive back without her. I couldn't help feeling like, *What am I doing here?* I mean, I didn't know Tina and Henry all that well, and Sarah and I were friendly and everything, but it wasn't like we were friends the way Laura and I were (or had been) friends, like it's totally normal that I'd be staying at her house for days (or even weeks) on end. Thinking about Laura made me feel kind of bad for how I hadn't wanted to hear about her and Brad very much. I mean, if there's one thing I'd learned from my . . . thing with Adam, it was that liking people makes you lose your mind a little.

"Would you like to come stay in the main house now that your mom's gone?" asked Tina as we pulled into the driveway.

"You mean so I won't fall victim to the local serial killer?"

She turned off the engine. "You know, I just thought it would be nice to have you closer. But when you put it like that, I guess it's imperative that you relocate immediately."

I was really glad she'd asked me to move. Despite my having freaked out at the idea of sharing a room with my mom when we first arrived, the idea of not sharing the guesthouse with her (or with anyone, for that matter) was even freakier. I threw my stuff into my suitcase and dragged it up the path and over to Tina and Henry's.

The guest room was on the third floor of the house, all by itself with its own little bathroom. It was tiny. There were sloping walls, a ceiling that wouldn't have allowed a grown man to stand up straight, and barely enough square footage for a single bed and a narrow chest of drawers. But the second I saw it I fell in love. It totally made me think of a writer's garret, and from the bed you could see out the window over the tops of the trees to the bay. On the dresser was a glossy coffee table book called *The Beaches of Cape Cod* and a stack of beautiful cream-colored note cards, each with a line drawing of the Dryer's Cove town hall. Tina gave me fresh sheets and towels, and after I'd made the bed, I just sat on it, wrapped up in the brightly colored patchwork quilt, looking out at the view.

"Hey, hey, hey," said Sarah, simultaneously knocking on and pushing open my door.

"Hi," I said. I hadn't even heard her car pull into the driveway.

"Hi," she said, and even though she already had, she asked, "can I come in?"

"Sure," I said.

"Your mom called me at work and said good-bye," she said, sitting down on the edge of the bed. "She left so fast."

"Yeah. I think it's some kind of make-or-break time."

"Intense. Are you okay?"

I crossed my legs so she would have more room to sit. "Yeah, I guess."

"Do you want to watch a movie at Jenna's later?"

I remembered the amazing dinner we'd all eaten there. Had it only been a few nights ago? "Who's going?"

I was relieved that Sarah knew exactly what I meant. "Well, not Adam because, according to Lawrence, he's skipped town." I didn't feel like admitting to Sarah how and why I'd actually already acquired that particular tidbit of information, so I just nodded. "And not David Carpenter, because I totally cannot face him. That's why Jenna and I didn't go to The Shack last night." For the first time since I'd known her, Sarah looked acutely embarrassed. Her face blushed pink and she lifted her shoulders and shuddered. "Ugh," she added.

I didn't exactly want to talk about David Carpenter, but at least Sarah had said she *didn't* want to see him. Which seemed a little strange given how crushed out she was on him. "Why can't you face David?" I asked. Thinking about it, I really couldn't picture Sarah with the guy I'd seen on the porch that morning. When she'd described him as outdoorsy and manly, I'd pictured someone a little less . . . Grizzly Adams.

She shook her head. "It's too embarrassing."

"Tell me."

She turned to me, opened her mouth, and then shut it immediately. "Can't."

Maybe she knew something really awful about him, something I could use to blackmail him. *Breathe one word to your brother about what I said to you and I'll tell everyone about. . . .* I leaned toward Sarah and took her shoulders in my hands. "Sarah, I'm not kidding. You have got to tell me why you can't face David Carpenter."

"Aaaah," yelped Sarah, thrusting me off her and curling up at the other end of the bed with her head as far away from me as she could get it. Suddenly she started speaking really fast. "Because last time I saw him was at our friend's graduation party in New York, and I'd had all this champagne and I told him I was totally in love with him." As soon as she finished her sentence, she whimpered and buried her head under a throw pillow.

240 "It's too awful."

I couldn't believe it. "Oh my God," I said.

"What?" she asked, lifting her face. "You can't believe what a loser I am, right?"

"Hardly," I said. I couldn't look at her so I dropped my eyes to the quilt and started pulling at a loose string. "This is going to sound *totally* impossible, but—"

"Yes . . ." she prompted.

"The exact same thing happened to me."

Her face was the picture of confusion. "You told David Carpenter you loved him?"

"Yes," I said. "But it's not what you think."

By the time I finished relating the story of my morning run, Sarah and I were both under the quilt.

"You know what this means, don't you?" asked Sarah.

"Neither of us can leave the house until Labor Day?"

"Exactly," she said. "I'm calling Jenna. I'll tell her it's safer if she comes here tonight."

"Good plan," I said. Sarah stood up and grabbed her shoes off the floor. "Tell her to bring provisions," I added as she went out the door.

"Most definitely," said Sarah. "At least a month's worth."

Now that I'd told Sarah what had happened with David that morning, it didn't seem nearly so bad as it had before. It was as if telling David Carpenter you were in love with him, purposely or mistakenly, was a rite of passage, something akin to failing your driver's test or 241 getting caught cheating on a Spanish test. Sure it's embarrassing and awful, but it happens to everyone.

And even though I knew Sarah had been joking about our spending the entire summer locked in her house, it was pretty cool how she hadn't minded the plan—like being forced to hang out with me for the next few weeks didn't bother her at all.

In fact, she'd kind of seemed to like the idea.

Chapter 24

THE FIRST THING I DID when I woke up the next morning was start working on my story. I only had a day to finish it, or at least get it to the point where I wouldn't mind showing it to someone. I wrote for over two hours, and when I stopped it wasn't because I'd run out of ideas but because my phone rang. When I saw it was Meg, my heart stopped. What if our parents had made some kind of decision and called her first?

"Hey," I said.

"I don't know anything," she said. "Do you?"

"Nothing," I said. I realized it was stupid to think something had already been decided. My mom hadn't even landed in Salt Lake yet.

"Ugh," she said. "This is driving me crazy."

"Totally," I said.

"I'm thinking about coming up to Cape Cod next week."

"You are?"

"Well, my class is over on Thursday and then I'm

just . . . hanging around here. And New York sucks in summer. Nobody's here."

"Sure," I said. "That's because they're all here."

Meg laughed. "Anyway, Tina invited me, so if it's okay with you, I think I'll come."

It was cool how my mom and my sister had both asked what I wanted for the rest of my summer. I mean, I'm not sure that Meg would have said okay if I'd said *Don't come*, but still—at least she pretended it was up to me.

"Yeah, sure," I said. "It would be great if you came." I wasn't totally lying either. If something was going to go down with our parents, I wanted Meg to be in the room with me when I heard about it.

"Okay," she said. "I'll check train schedules and let you guys know in the next couple of days."

"Great," I said. "I'll talk to you soon."

Talking to Meg made me feel antsy. What was going to happen to my family?

I walked to the window and back to the bed, but the room wasn't exactly big enough for serious pacing. The second time I crossed it, my eyes landed on the pile of note cards in the basket, and I remembered that before leaving Salt Lake City I'd promised to write Laura a postcard every day. It was as if I'd made that promise in a different lifetime. Should I call her? If I waited any longer to fill her in on what was happening in my life, we'd run through all my minutes for the rest of the year. Where would I start? Adam? My parents? Brad?

I grabbed a card off the top of the pile and opened it. *This town has witnessed the most bizarre/awful experiences of my life*, I wrote. *Call me when you have at least ten hours to talk.* And then I added, *I miss you.* Writing her name and address on the envelope felt good. Familiar. And it was true. I did miss Laura.

I showered and dressed and went downstairs, carrying the card with me. I'd bring it to the post office later. Nobody was home and I stood on the porch and ate a banana, looking out at the view. It was a gorgeous sunny day, the sky a crisp bright blue, with a just a few clouds floating high above me. It was so perfect that if someone had shown me a painting of the scene, I would have said it was clichéd.

I headed down to the beach and sat on the warm sand, remembering how at one time the view had creeped me out. Now it made me feel calm.

Looking out at the water, I tried not to think about what was going to happen with my parents. There was nothing I could do about it either way. I stretched out my back, reaching my arms up to the sky. And there was nothing I could do about Adam either. As I made my way up the path to the house I accepted reality: David would tell Adam what I'd said, Adam would think I was a loser, we'd avoid each other until I left, end of story.

Only Lady Brett Ashley gets to be Lady Brett Ashley.

There was one problem, though. If Adam and I were going to avoid each other for the rest of the summer, what was he doing standing on the deck of the Cooper-Melnick house?

I'd gotten almost to the stairs before I saw him.

"Hi," he said.

"Hi," I said. He was wearing a flannel shirt and jeans and hiking boots that appeared to actually have been hiked in, and he looked so cute it made my throat ache. I realized David hadn't lost any time telling Adam what I'd told him. Clearly Adam had decided it was only fair to come by and explain that I should probably get over him since he'd been in New Hampshire reconciling with his girlfriend.

"So, can I tell you the weirdest thing?" he said, and he sat down on the top step.

"Um, sure," I said, even though I'd had more than my fair share of weird lately.

"Okay, I went up to New Hampshire to—"

Did he think nobody had told me Molly was in New Hampshire for the summer? "I know why you went to New Hampshire," I said.

"You do?" he said, genuinely surprised.

"More or less," I said. Was there any way I could pretend I'd never said those things to David? When you

246

came down to it, it was David's word against mine. Then again, why would David make up a story like that? *Dude, I don't know. Clearly your brother has something* seriously *wrong with him.* The silence stretched out between us.

"Um, when did you get home?" I asked. He really hadn't been gone very long. Suddenly a terrible thought occurred to me: could he have gone to New Hampshire to pick Molly up and bring her to Cape Cod? I remembered Jenna and Sarah talking the day of the whale watch. *I think she's probably coming up in August like usual.* My stomach lurched.

"I haven't even been home yet," said Adam. "I just came straight here."

Wait . . . was it possible David hadn't said anything about our "conversation" yesterday? I gave Adam a long look, trying to figure out what exactly he knew. But he was looking past me at the water over my shoulder.

"Oh," I said. If he didn't know yet, I could play it cool, pretend everything between us was just fine, that I'd ended things because I just wasn't into him anymore. "Well, it's . . . it's great to see you."

"Why am I not believing you?" he asked.

Okay, this was completely hopeless. Even if he hadn't heard about what I'd said to David yet, he would soon. "What do you want, Adam? Why are you here? I know you went to New Hampshire to get back together with Molly."

Adam suddenly burst out laughing, but I didn't exactly see what was so funny, and I didn't feel like talking to him anymore. I turned to go the long way around so I could get into the house by the side door.

"Wait," he said. "Please. Wait."

In spite of myself, I stopped.

"Look," he said, "I don't know what you think you know, but . . . I did go to New Hampshire to see Molly."

I turned to face him. "And you're telling me this because . . ."

"Because I thought you might like to know that the reason I drove to New Hampshire to see Molly was that I thought it wasn't nice to break up with her on the phone."

"You—"

"And then last night, when I was on the first night of what turned out to be the world's shortest solo fishing trip, my brother called and told me some girl had told him she was really into him, only he had this idea that maybe she was really saying she was into *me*."

We looked at each other.

"You broke up with Molly?"

"I broke up with Molly."

I squinted at him suspiciously. "Why did you break up with Molly?"

"Because I knew I really liked you. And I figured even

if you didn't like me back, I couldn't get back together

with Molly when I'd met another girl I liked as much as I liked you."

Was this really happening? This couldn't really be happening. "Wait," I said. "Why didn't you tell me you liked me if you liked me so much? I mean, why didn't you tell me before?"

Adam looked down at the porch step, and as he toyed with a long splinter of wood, I was reminded of myself on the deck with David. "Why didn't *you* tell *me* you liked *me* if you liked me so much?" he asked finally, still picking at the pale gray wood.

"I did," I said. "I mean, I tried to. I just told the wrong guy."

Adam stopped studying the step and looked up at me. "I was embarrassed, okay? It's hard to say what you feel. Especially when the other person says she doesn't want to, you know, hang out with you anymore."

I couldn't help smiling. "Hang out? That's pretty lame, Carpenter."

He ran his fingers through his hair and groaned. "Are you gonna cut me some slack here or what?"

"Oh, I don't know," I said, folding my arms and cocking my head at him. "I mean, do I really want a boyfriend who needs me to cut him slack?"

Adam crossed his arms and stared back at me. "I have other qualities," he said.

"Such as?" I asked.

He thought for a second. "I'm a pretty good tennis player," he said.

"Negative," I said. "As I remember that game, I kicked your ass."

"True," he acknowledged. Then he said, "I'm a decent kisser."

I could feel myself blush, both at what he'd said and at the memory of kissing him.

"Oh really?" I pretended to be thinking, then said, "I can't quite recall."

"Might I be so bold as to offer to refresh your memory?"

"Oh, I suppose," I said.

He was down the stairs in a matter of seconds, and our arms were around each other and we were kissing. Each time one of us went to pull away, the other would pull the person back. The kiss seemed to last forever.

Finally we came up for air.

"Not bad," I said. "Not bad at all." My vision was blurry and my voice shook.

"Hey," he said, like he'd just thought of something, "why did you think I'd come here?" He kissed his way up my jaw.

"I thought you were paying . . . I don't know, a courtesy call or something," I said, only half thinking about the words as I felt his lips on my ear.

Keeping his arms around my waist, he pulled

away. "A courtesy call?! What are we, in a Jane Austen novel?"

When he put it that way, I had to admit my idea had been a little nuts. I shrugged.

He shook his head. "I don't know, Draper," he said. "Do I really need a girlfriend who's certifiably crazy?"

I pulled him to me, and we kissed again, melting into each other. "You're right," I said into his lips. "Maybe we should just, you know, hang out. You're not looking for some big serious thing, are you?"

"You're hilarious," he said, running his hand up my back. "I hope you're prepared for me to come skiing in Salt Lake this Christmas."

"I just hope you ski better than you play tennis," I said, digging my hands into his hair.

"I'm a great skier," he said. "Expert. You'll see. Maybe I couldn't beat you at tennis, but I vow to leave you in the dust as we make our way down the mountain."

"Oh, Adam," I said, laughing. "Isn't it pretty to think so?"

As I said the words, Adam's lips met mine again, and I realized that for the first time ever, I didn't wish I could feel the way Lady Brett Ashley did.

I wished, for her sake, that she could feel like me.

Acknowledgments

This book and its author have relied heavily on the kindness of friends and strangers whose generosity cannot be overstated. Thank you, Jennifer Besser, Donna Bray, Rebecca Friedman, Benjamin Gantcher, Bernie Kaplan, and Helen Perelman.